Rise of a D-List Supervillain

by

Jim Bernheimer

First Printing: Createspace August 2017

Print ISBN: 197585005X

Print ISBN-13: 978-1975850050

Dedication and Acknowledgements

I'm astounded that people are not only reading this, but they are asking me for more.

Mind boggling. It truly is.

Obviously, the first person I have to thank is my lovely wife, Kim. She puts up with listening to all the odd scenes that come to mind (usually with very little context) just so I can see if she likes the one liner at the end.

She has a lot of patience.

I'll thank my girls, Laura and Marissa next. All those questions about what I'm writing and if this is a book that they can read. Laura, yes. Marissa, not for another four years. Let Daddy cling to the idea that you're still young and innocent for a bit longer.

Jeffrey Kafer does a magnificent job narrating this series. If you're reading this, you should stop and give him a listen before continuing. He's a large part of the success of this series and I am grateful that David Wood introduced us all those years ago. David got me started by being my publisher and has shared much of his knowledge know that I'm publishing other people.

Then there are the people who gave this a test read – Flora Demuth, David Bagini, Graham Adizma, Amanda Rae Westfal, Charles Phipps, and Michael Gibson. The story is that much better for your input. Tara Ellis and Valerie Kann get a special thanks for all the editing work. The story is MUCH better because of your hard work. Seriously, my grammar and punctuation borders on the abysmal.

Now, I need to thank the fans. From the folks who still contact me and ask me if I'm going to write a sequel to a fanfic to those that ask about the next *Spirals of Destiny* novel. (It's my next project. I promise!) You guys and girls bump into me at conventions or contact me on my website and Facebook. I get such a kick out of interacting with you. Special thanks to Dave Evans, Grigory Lukin, Megan Bostic, Alec Vendura, Caitlyn Merchant, and Steve Caldwell. You rock!

Special Note from the Author

In *Horror, Humor, and Heroes Volume IV*, I published a five chapter Hillbilly Bobby novella called *Thugs, Lies, and Spies*. In chronological order, that work starts when Bobby left the base to go do some work/spy on The Apostle during *Secrets of a D-List Supervillain*. The first chapter of this novel covers the same basic material from Cal Stringel's point of view as the final chapter in Bobby's novella. You will also see some things from that story mentioned in passing (Bobby fighting Seawall and federal agents at a Manglermal brothel, his adoption of a fake identity, The Highwayman, among other things) during this story.

So, if you ever wanted to read about this universe from Bobby's point of view, you are more than welcome to check it and the other short stories in the collection.

Rise of a D-List Supervillain

Chapter One

Rednecks, and Tigers, and Imposters, Oh My!

"What's the word, Andy?" I ask, sliding into the chair and jacking into the Megasuit.

"Hello Cal," the android replies. "Your armor is currently on a shuttered oil rig eighteen miles away from Bobby's last reported position. I am attempting to get a visual on the Port of New Orleans, but E.M. Pulsive seems to be generating an inordinate amount of electrical interference at this time. Based on reports, the assembled group of villains appears to be attacking the cargo ships docked there. Local police are establishing a perimeter and the Gulf Coast Guardians are currently en route. Their ETA is five minutes."

I hadn't cared for Bobby's "I'm gonna go spy on what the bad guys are doing" plans when he first started doing them, and I didn't like it now.

"Doesn't fit Eddie's way of doing things," I mutter, referring to Pulsive's actions. "He doesn't usually advertise his presence until he is ready to leave. It looks like they just got there."

Bobby hadn't been in contact for over two days, but with Eddie involved, it was easy to see why. The electrical supervillain might be able to intercept the signals.

"Have you been able to tap into camera feeds in the area?"

"Not yet. The Port's cameras appear to be on a closed circuit and not accessible from our current position. A search of contracts awarded indicates that the system is twelve years old."

"Well, that sucks donkey balls!" I say, cursing outdated technology. Security by obscurity giving me the digital finger and all that crap.

Andydroid glances at me. "I concur with your colorful assessment of the situation. It is less than optimal. Object detected en route to Port of New Orleans. Displaying on screen three."

I look at where Andy indicates. It's from the outside of a liquor store using the default passwords for their wireless CCTV setup. "Is that a knockoff of my old Roller? No. There's a windshield. Blow it up for me, would ya?"

The resolution is crappy, but I make out that someone is inside, and the blurry markings tell me who it is. "Holy shit! The Bugler built the DCV we drew up the plans for back in the day!"

The Biloxi Bugler, also known as Bo Carr, and I had a fairly complicated history. My stint in prison at his hands, and my putting his ass in the hospital, had been sore point to get over. I nearly crapped my pants when he and I ended up on the Gulf Coast Guardians during my not-so-successful attempt at going legit.

Somewhere along the way, I started to respect him. Bo, in his mid-fifties, would go out there with no real powers other than the sonic bugle he'd invented and "play the high notes of justice."

Back when I couldn't scrounge enough synth to replace a set of powered armor together and he had been recovering from both his legs being broken, Bo and I tossed around the idea of a new identity for me, The Dronemaster. Instead of armor, we would build a set of robots that would be operated from a Drone Control Vehicle.

The object on the screen, decked out with the state flag of Mississippi, looks a lot like the plans the two of us drew up, before I faked my death. It evokes a mixture of feelings—envy that Bo built it and I didn't, pride that Bo pulled it off, and a bit of disappointment that I won't be able to get inside of it anytime soon and check it out.

Who knew that pretending to be dead could actually have a downside?

I make a note to mention this to my girlfriend to impress her with my ever-expanding depth of character. Naturally, she will reply that I am telling her this to convince her to slip away from her team of Olympians for a booty call, which will negate the personal development I plan to project.

Especially since I would be trying to convince her to visit at that time.

I will need to prepare a good counterargument, I think while disengaging the Gepetto Interface so I can drink a bottle of water without having Megasuit duplicate my actions.

Along with the Post-it note attached to the bottom of the monitor with the words *Anything you are doing, the armor is too!* scribbled on it, the marks on the rear plating from that time I really had to scratch my ass serve as a constant reminder.

"Do you have a visual on Bobby yet? Think I should move closer to the action?"

Andy continues monitoring his feeds, but answers without looking at me. "There is no indication that your position is compromised. The only reason to alter that is if you believe our double agent is in jeopardy. The likelihood of Bobby Walton's death or severe injury in a confrontation with our former team is minimal. His capture is a greater possibility, but if the armor is spotted, questions will be asked as to why we did not take an active role in the skirmish."

Andy makes too much damn sense sometimes.

Maybe I'm just spoiling for a fight. After all those times Eddie used to goad and threaten me, it would be hilarious to see him shit a high-voltage brick when faced with the Megasuit.

Unfortunately, Andy is right. My own petty need for a pound of flesh, or joule of energy in this case, isn't worth putting our operation on the line.

Eddie's smug ass just isn't worth it. He's chum that will hopefully lead us to bigger fish. There was a time when I thought he was better than me. I was wrong. I'm more than a guy whose gift is inventing things and a dabbler in ancient dinosaur magic. Eddie is much less than the sum of his electrical powers. We've both killed people in the commission of crimes, but Eddie would kill anyone in his path without a second thought. I rarely lose sleep over killing someone, but there are only a few people I'd go out of my way to off.

See! Now that's personal growth. I just have to figure out how to use it.

As the minutes tick by, Andy gives me as much detail as he can scrounge, but Pulsive has that section of New Orleans lit up like a Christmas tree.

Garbled bits of 911 dispatches come in, while the local news channel states that they are intentionally keeping their helicopter out of the area for the safety of the crew. Considering the way Eddie operates, I don't blame them.

"I think it's about time we bring the boss lady up to speed. How 'bout you?"

"I have already sent her a message with a summary of the situation at this time. Wendy's response directs that we should continue to monitor and that I should try to prevent you from doing anything stupid. I am in the process of replying that there are too many independent variables to account for all the stupid courses of action you are capable of."

"Are you making fun of me?" I ask Andy.

"It is merely an observation of the behavior patterns you demonstrate and your penchant for plans that succeed while defying the low probabilities I calculate. No offense is intended, Cal."

His disclaimer makes me more suspicious that he is making fun of me. That's the problem with having on my team the most advanced artificial lifeform I'd ever met.

The New Renegades are a dysfunctional, but merry, band of misfits. WhirlWendy, America's sweetheart, with over a decade in the superhero business, is our leader. She gave her childhood and teenage years in dutiful service to being a hero. What did it get her? The adoration of the public? Yeah, sure. It also taught her how callous and uncaring those in power could be. The government propaganda cannons are targeted on Wendy right now, and her own father's fingers are on the trigger.

Wendy LaGuardia has multiple reasons for being upset. Half the time the reasons are connected back to me in some way or another. We decided early on to not play by the rules, and the people opposed to change are pushing back. Our team name might need to change to the New Fugitives.

"Anything on Bobby yet?" Larry Hitt asks, descending the staircase into *my domain*. He's a stocky man, with short black hair and a hint of gray starting to creep in, which is sad because of all the years our team's version of Rip Van Winkle had lost.

"Just that he's about to throw down with the Gulf Coasters."

"Need me to suit up?" He gestures to his shorts and tee shirt.

"Not yet, but be on standby," I answer as best I can.

"Pulsive has increased his electromagnetic interference," Andy announces. "It is outside of his normal operating parameters. It is beginning to cause problems with transmissions across the spectrum."

Larry looks confused until I explain, "Eddie did something similar a few years back, when he tried to shake down a TV network by jamming game seven of the World Series. Unless he's had a boost that we haven't heard about, he can only maintain it for ten minutes."

Part of me resists the urge to make some kind of performance joke at the expense of the villain, but I decide to take the higher road, or maybe just the road not taken. Either way, I let it go and focus on the matter at hand.

"Eddie has already been paid," I say, "so there is no money in this for him. Since we can't find any specific cargo he is targeting, Eddie and the rest of his crew must be there just to cause destruction. The real question is why there, and what can they gain from it?"

"Perhaps it is a distraction? Bobby did say that Eddie enticed him with a chance to fight his cousin and our former teammate," Andy offers. He got along with Sheila when we were on the Gulf Coast Guardians. Her low opinion of me mirrored the one I had of her. We frequently challenged each other to do things that were anatomically impossible, and not in a good-natured manner, either.

I nod my head at my mechanical buddy, because that's the only thing that makes a damn bit of sense. "Any idea what else someone might be after in New Orleans while the resident super team is otherwise occupied?"

Andy tosses out several theories, including bank robberies, political kidnappings, hijackings, and a few things I could barely wrap my mind around. He then rattles off all the reasons why we can discount most of these theories.

With a frown, I flip a toggle switch that sends a signal through a small fragment of a magic mirror and turns on a little light in Stacy Mitchell's suit of powered armor. If she is in her armor and sees it, she will switch to a private channel and talk with me.

Roughly thirty seconds pass before I hear her charming voice coming through the speakers. She could read street directions and make them sound sexy! "Hey, Cal. What's up?"

"The Gulf Coasters are fighting E.M. Pulsive and his crew. I don't know if word has reached you yet."

"No," she says. "I'm in the Philippines trying to track down a local who may or may not have a connection to Mount Pinatubo."

"I could see how that might be a problem. Piss the dude off and volcano go boom. You working with backup?"

"It's a her, and no," she responds. "She's a fifteen-year-old girl and not a villain. I'm widely considered the most harmless Olympian after Hestia. Well, except for just after your book was released. Sadly, things have gone back to normal."

In fairness, we were on a break when I wrote my "tell-all," but I wasn't very charitable to her. The fact that she doesn't hold it against me is pretty damn amazing.

"Is Hestia's chip on her shoulder as big as yours? If the public only knew," I say and laugh. "You are definitely not harmless. I have bruises too, for proof."

"Aw, poor baby. Are you trying to say that I'm more woman than you can handle? Why didn't you say something?"

She teases, but I'm not having it. "I think it's more a case that I drive you so crazy that you can't control yourself. Because that's how I roll!"

"You're pretty full of yourself today," the Olympian retorts.

"I'm just shocked that you're actually using your armor on a real mission. That alone is worth a celebration. Do you have a picture of volcano girl? I could have Andy scour the social websites for any sign of her."

"Yes. Give me a second and I'll push it across our link. The wireless is pretty slow, though. Who do I have to sleep with to get an upgrade?"

"Next time we can set up a meet, I can install a more powerful transmitter. That old fifty-four meg one was all I had on hand. Besides, I didn't expect you to be using your armor anytime soon."

"Cal, you're not going to be happy unless I'm in this thing eighteen hours a day," she replies after a slight chuckle.

"Bah! I'd settle for twelve," I say as the photo comes across our wireless. Andy snatches it from my screen before I even get a good look at the young lady Stacy is searching for. It makes me wonder if her Aphrodite powers actually do work on my android buddy.

He has been going on about relationships lately and roleplaying with his two robots. I'm probably just being paranoid, or more paranoid than I usually am. Flora asked me why I am such a hot mess last time the robot was down here. Oh well, if it makes Andy happy to play with mechanical dolls...

Pushing that odd train of thought onto a different track, I ask, "So when do you think you can slip away from those turds who are holding you back?"

"Oh, you mean my team? They are my friends, you know. Considering I have to put up with Bobby, you could be a bit more charitable. Cecil is taking up sculpting. He wants me to pose for him when he gets better."

"Hephaestus? Probably wants you to do a nude. His wife probably wouldn't appreciate that."

The original Hephaestus, who left the island with Stacy and her cohorts, died on their second mission when he tried to handle Fiery Doom by his lonesome. His brother inherited the Olympian power and replaced him. Cecil was the only member of the Olympians that was married.

All the rest are the hottest singles on the market, especially my girlfriend.

"Nah, Cecil wants to sculpt me in my armor with my helmet off."

I reset my internal paranoia meter back to the regular level of **"They're out to get me!"**

We continue to chitchat for at least ten more minutes until Wendy uses the intercom to ask everyone to meet in central command in her cheerful "Now!" voice.

"Gotta run upstairs for a few and see what the boss lady is upset about. Good luck with Volcano Girl. Call you back in a few."

"Tell Wendy I said hi," she says as I turn over control of Mega to Andy and disconnect. The two of them are cordial enough, but there is always this slightly off feeling whenever my lover and my baby mama are in the same room.

Sometimes I almost think it is jealousy. Stacy's powers bring that out in women. It kind of goes with the whole Love Goddess theme. Mostly, I believe that Wendy sees Stacy as something that distracts me from being both a better father to Gabby or as a member of the team.

I wind the disconnected cables up, strap them to my puppeteer suit, and climb the steps. At the top, I throw open the door and say, "You summoned me, oh bitchy one?"

"Holy shit! Cal Stringel!" someone says in a deep voice.

Standing next to the short, Italian-American superhero is a six-foot-six, hulking Bengal tiger/human hybrid wearing a tuxedo. He has Gabby in his arms and she is happily tugging on his facial fur.

"You two headed out on a date or something? I'm kinda in the middle of an op, but I can babysit," I ask, masking my surprise at seeing Paper Tiger. Wendy drops hints every so often that she wants to bring him on to our little dysfunctional squad, but I thought I'd get at least a heads up out of common courtesy. We could have at least baked a cake or come up with a new member hazing routine.

Damn! Now I want cake.

"Cut the shit, Cal!" Wendy snaps. "He's here because Bobby let the cat out of the bag, so don't go looking at me like that!"

I honestly am not looking at her "like that." I am still thinking about what kind of cake I can talk Andy into making tonight. "What happened?"

The animated drawing possessed by Wendy's boyfriend answers, "Your associate figured out that the fight at the port was just a distraction and the real target was my team's headquarters. It was Apostle's people."

There are several surprising things in Paper Tiger's sentence. Bobby figuring something out is one. The other is someone wanting to attack the beat-up old former high school and National Guard armory that serves as the home for the Gulf Coasters.

"What were you storing there?"

"Not a damn thing. All they did was kidnap José."

"Can one of his clones tell you where they are taking him?"

"Pulsive killed them all. Looked like he was doing it on purpose, too."

José Six-Pack and I used to be on good terms—at least as much as I ever get along with the heroes. His power to make five copies of himself wasn't all that spectacular. It just meant there were six normal guys who could think like one person. Excluding Stacy, José and Bo qualify as the closest thing to actual friends I had during my stint as a Gulf Coaster. Hell! He even offered to set me up with one of his cousins when Stacy dumped my sorry ass.

Granted, Rosita wasn't a very good-looking cousin, but considering the miserable sack of whiny crap I was at that time and that my own looks aren't exactly in the top tier either, it counted in my book. Unfortunately, Lazarus Patterson sent a bunch of robots to kill me, and she was dating someone else by the time I got back on my feet. Things worked out in the end and for that I'm grateful.

Returning to the matter at hand, I ask, "Are you going to attempt a rescue?"

"We're not sure where to start," Tiger admitted. "False Idol mind controlled him and José locked down our main systems and power grid, while the telekinetic and the strongman trashed the place. Plus, we're licking our wounds from the fight at the docks. I'm hoping you guys can help."

My jaw clenches while I weigh the risk. Wendy doesn't hesitate. "We're in."

José was her teammate, too. She was the one who promoted him from being the groundskeeper and security guard for the Gulf Coasters to regular member.

The main screen shifts and Andy's face appears. "Bobby is requesting an extraction. I have instructed him to remain hidden at his present location."

"Cal," she commands. "Pick up the dumbass and send him back through the suit. Since everyone thinks Mega is Andy, he can take it to Gulf Coast HQ and break the lock on the computers and get the power grid back up. Maybe we can get a lead from whatever the surveillance cameras caught. Since False Idol is influencing him, we can't count on José giving us any breadcrumbs to follow."

"Understood. I am going to run back to my portrait at HQ and check on things," Paper Tiger says and looks at me. "I should be more surprised that you're alive, but your secret is safe with me, Mr. Stringel."

"Call me Cal," I say.

"Charles," he replies and hands Gabby back to Wendy, minus the fur she'd been pulling from his face. He leans down and nuzzles against Wendy's cheek before heading back into her bedroom.

I wait thirty seconds for him to transfer back into the portrait frame. Charles has a weird power to draw human/tiger hybrids and make them come to life. The drawings can have wings, be cyborgs, and have all kinds of weapons, but they always have to be hybrids of humans and tigers. It isn't especially powerful, but he can travel through his frames to anywhere that has a sketch or painting. It gives him unmatched mobility and the power to be on the other side of the world in less than a minute. He's almost as much of a recluse as I am turning out to be.

Introverts of the world unite! But don't interact with each other!

Like I said, pretty weird. If I had his powers, with my "artistic talent," I would have odd, stick-figure-looking cat blobs. It wouldn't be pretty.

• • •

After installing the fake Andy head inside of Mega, I land my suit in the back alley of a strip mall and watch Bobby come out from behind a dumpster, where he had waited for his ride. From the look on his face, he seems pleased with himself.

I can't say the same thing. My secret is now in the hands of someone I barely know, and he's another hero. I don't know if his mind can be read when Charles merges with a picture. We only have two more mind blockers and he might not be able to use them.

Watching Bobby squeeze his huge frame out of the largest teleportation mirror fragment, I cringe in fear that he'll break it. It's not like I have another to replace it. Plus, there is always the unfortunate discovery that these fragments are vulnerable to magic. That doesn't help me rest easy. My supersuit, something I bragged could be the most powerful thing on the planet, has a massive glass jaw. I know enough magic to be dangerous—to myself. To protect my technological baby, I created some defenses that worked in a test environment. I'm not eager to see how they work in the real world.

"Welcome back," I say. "The others are waiting for us upstairs."

"You been feeding my animals, like you promised?"

Bobby's small zoo is annoying. One of the ferrets is a damn escape artist. "Andy has."

"So any idea what's going on?"

I try to come up with a suitable answer, but Bobby spots Paper Tiger, who must have finished his errands. "Oh, he's here now. Long time no see."

Wendy lit into him. "What'd you expect would happen when you told him you were working with us?"

"You're always saying what a good guy he is, and I couldn't exactly get in contact with you with no phone. I made a call and trusted a hero that you keep saying we should trust. Deal with it."

There's an awkward pause after Bobby's statement. Paper Tiger breaks it by offering his paw. "Charles Phipps."

Bobby takes it, and asks how his cousin, She-Dozer, is. He actually seems sort of concerned. I find that odd. He hates Sheila, like close to how much I hate Lazarus Patterson.

Maybe I'm not the only experiencing a personal growth spurt.

Of the people—well, lifeforms, since there is an android and possessed piece of artwork here too, in the room—Wendy looks the least happy, while Charles brings Bobby up to date on José's abduction. It makes me wonder how invested she is in her relationship with Paper Tiger. Any time Stacy came around, Wendy would always mention that she should bring Charles here—and now he is.

Are his drawings anatomically . . . No Cal! Don't go there. Probably better not to ask.

As Bobby makes a snide remark about how worthless José's powers are, I am stuck thinking about Wendy's control issues.

That's when it hits me! Control! Sonofabitch! That's why. "A control. Shit! They need him for a control. You told us Apostle is working with Devious and Doc Mangler. They're going to experiment on José!"

Andy backs me up. "It is a plausible scenario. He is the only known individual capable of producing a stable clone. Perhaps Doctor. Mangler is preparing to test a new protocol in his Improved Human Procedure? It is also possible that he may be testing a method for creating multiple Manglermals at the same time."

I don't like that theory any more than the rest of the group.

"All right, here's what," Wendy starts.

"I think we should—" Larry says at the same time.

"What about—" I contribute to the verbal mayhem.

Everyone stops when they realize how stupid we all sound.

Tiger is the first to get out something we can understand. "Mangler has been operating out of Mexico and Central America according to the folks I know at Interpol. I've got one of my sketches in Mexico City and can drop in on K-Otica and Spirit Staff there. They might have some information."

I nod. Both were former Gulf Coasters when I used to be a bad guy. They should be willing to help a former team member out.

"I can put out feelers on VillainNet, acting like things are getting too hot up this way, to see what kind of jobs are happening down that away," Bobby says, shocking damn near everyone in the room. "Might tell us more than those two ex-Gulf Coasters ever could."

Wendy's eyes are almost as big as saucers, but she replies, "Good idea, Bobby. Run with it."

For his part, Bobby has this look on his face like he ate something that didn't agree with him. He seems a little different, coming back from his spying mission, and I file it away to talk with him about it later. Now just doesn't seem like the right time. He wanders away from the center table and heads for the couch, where several beers and an endless variety of television wait for him.

We toss around a couple of scenarios that look promising. From the corner of my eye, I see Wendy frown as Bobby abandons the conversation.

"The only one out of Bobby's group who knows what is going on is Pulsive," Wendy states. "Do you think we should hunt him down?"

"Maybe," I reply. "Any one of the three of us can take him, though I'm not really sure whether Larry's TK can affect Eddie in his electrical form."

Larry scratches the scruff on his chin. "If I can't directly hold him, I'll dump a pond on top of him or wrap him up in metal and short him out."

I want to smile as my mind pictures Larry with Eddie wrapped in steel, telling him that he's "grounded." Larry's come a long way from when I put that necklace around his neck and brought his insane power down to a slightly less insane level. He's beginning to think beyond the direct attacks and how to use his power as more than just a battering ram.

If our fight happened two years from now, I probably wouldn't be able to stop him without using the gauss cannon. Good thing he's on my side.

"I can talk to Stacy and see if she can get Zeus down here. Eddie's Achilles heel is his fear of that particular Olympian."

That piques Paper Tiger's curiosity. "So Aphrodite knows you're still alive?"

"Yeah."

"And you're .. ."

"Like bunnies."

"I was going to say back together, but I guess that covers it. Good for you two, then!"

The cynic in me senses his relief, since he's obviously wondering where Wendy and I stand. I could put him at ease and tell him we do our best to co-parent Gabby Gabby Doo and kick ass on the battlefield, but beyond that, I enjoy annoying her and she enjoys yelling at me. Granted, it is an odd system, but we make it work.

"All right," Wendy says. "Let's get back to the problem at hand. Let's get a jump on this before something else happens."

Not five seconds after Ms. Open-Her-Big-Fat-Mouth says that, Bobby hollers, "Hey, Cal! You might want to come see this. Someone's in California pretending to be you!"

I stop and can only stare at cell phone footage of a naked guy stumbling out of the water onto the beach. Mercifully, an onlooker tosses him a towel. The words below provided by the news station ask, **CAL STRINGEL ALIVE?**

"What happened to you, dude?" someone asks the person who looks too close to the guy staring at me in the bathroom mirror every morning.

"A damn nuclear explosion happened! Where's my team? I can't believe I lost another set of armor! Shit! Shit! Shit!"

Everyone is staring at me, waiting for my reaction. My mouth starts moving and I'm not sure what is going to come out.

"You've got to be fucking kidding me!"

Chapter Two

An Idea Millions of Years in the Making

"Aw," Bobby says. "You said the 'F' word!"

I'm in no mood for his shit. On the screen, there's a person who looks just like me, wrapped only in a beach towel, and trying to pass himself off as me. Never in a million years would I have suspected that someone would try and steal the shitty life I had back when I faked my death.

Things have improved since then, but seriously, what the flippin' hell?

"Cal, don't do anything rash," Wendy cautions.

All the eyes in the room are on me, waiting for me to flip out or something.

"It's not me," I pronounce and shake my head. "He asked about his team before mentioning his armor. Think about it."

Wendy LaGuardia laughs at my shallowness. "You're right. I don't think you stopped moaning about losing the damn set that was turned to stone until you had built a new one!"

"He still complains about it," Andydroid adds. "I recorded three instances in the previous month."

Everyone shares a laugh at my expense, except for Paper Tiger. Charles doesn't know me that well and isn't sure whether or not he should join in.

"So why aren't you already jacking into Mega for a trip to California?" Larry asks.

Wendy offers her opinion. "Because he is stupid under normal circumstances. It's like the angrier he gets, the smarter he gets. Plus, he knows I'd fucking stop him from going off half-assed like that."

Taking a deep breath along with her backhanded compliment, I try to explain. "We're either looking at a shapeshifter or a clone, Larry. A clone, unless they've perfected the process, requires all kinds of special equipment to stay alive. It's why that clone of Joe Ducie never stayed away from the Overlord's base for more than three days."

It's true. Clone Ducie started aging rapidly and pretty much fell apart after the Overlord's cloning equipment was destroyed. Damn shame too, because I liked the guy. When he died, it was almost a mercy death and left me wondering if clones had an afterlife. Of course, José's kidnapping at the same time this impostor arrives on the scene makes me curious if the two are connected. I'm too angry to get a good read on my gut instinct.

"I agree with Cal," Wendy states. "We know where the real Cal is. Thanks to the media, we will know everywhere that fake is pretty much every second of the day. The fake could be in it for the fame and money, or he's a plant for someone like Devious or the Overlord. What we don't know is where Apostle's people took José. He's our priority right now."

She heads off my objections with an open palm. "I'm not ignoring this. We just have to stay dialed in to our rescue mission. Whatever game the fake is playing will come out in the next few weeks. My hope is that we have the Six-Pack back by then and we can give this our full, undivided attention."

I yield the battlefield to her, but don't completely withdraw. "We're stacking up enemies pretty quick, between this crap, your father, and that shit the government is doing to try and duplicate Seawall's powers…"

"Huh?" Paper Tiger interrupts. "What's that about Seawall? We brought him in."

Wendy gives me a dirty look.

Guess she didn't want to get into that today. And today started off so nice and quiet. Oh, just deal with it, boss!

She looks at the tuxedo-wearing tiger man. "Bobby fought him in Nevada at that brothel."

"I heard about Bobby killing three federal agents there, but nothing about Seawall."

Bobby replies. It's his story to tell, anyway. "Seawall went and cut a lab rat deal. Uncle Sam's making this little patch, which instead of helping you quit smoking, gives you Seawall's powers for a minute. Guess they don't trust you heroes as much as they used to and are thinking 'bout taking matters into their own hands."

Phipps snarls a bit. "The government's always been on an Improved Human kick. It's what gave us the Manglermals in the first place."

The tough-talking tiger makes a point. There are at least a dozen countries out there running programs similar to this, but the idea of being swarmed over by a platoon of temporarily invulnerable commandos doesn't sit well with him either.

"And you fought Seawall there, too?"

"Sure as shit I did. Tossed his ass into the helicopter rotors and brought it down. Didn't kill his turncoat ass, but he's out of action for the time being. He did this glowy cocoon thing."

"It's all true, Charles," Wendy says. "He even brought back some samples of the patches they used. Andy is performing a detailed analysis of them."

Having enough of the present conversation, I announce, "I'm going down to see if I can get ahold of Stacy and let her know about this new development. Andy, what's the suit doing?"

"Still working at the Gulf Coast Guardians' compound. I am clearing debris and having a conversation with Sheila concerning the restart procedures for the base's power grid. She is not in a good mood. I believe Stacy has already learned of the news. Her light signaling the desire for conversation has been illuminated for ten minutes and thirty-seven seconds. I apologize for not informing you earlier, but I judged this conversation to be more pertinent."

"You can stay in control of the armor. Any day I don't have to talk to She-Dozer is a good day—except for today, it seems. Pump Stacy's feed to the downstairs screen. Maybe I can talk her into checking out the bastard impersonating me, but I'm guessing the people behind this have already taken into account most of the things that could debunk the fake."

• • •

"Holly contacted me," Stacy says. "Any idea what's going on?"

"Someone has a death wish," I say into my headset, while prodding a hollowed wooden cylinder that I have been carving runes into as part of my quest to protect my armor from magic. "Let me guess, Athena's not happy I'm alive. If she only knew!"

"She made several comments. I don't think it would be wise to repeat them. For my part, I tried not to sound too interested."

"OK, lay it on me. What did your BFF say?"

"Cal ..." A note of exasperation creeps into her voice.

"Oh, come on! You're always on me whenever I say something. I'm having a bad day, give me a little something here. I feed on her disappointment and pettiness."

"OK then, if you insist. She said assuming that is really you, it proves you're some form of cockroach since you can survive a nuclear blast. I told her that wasn't very nice."

"But she's such a nice person you always tell me," I say, verbally poking at her.

"Yeah, yeah, she hates you and you hate her. The big question is what are you going to do about this person claiming to be you?"

"As much as I would like to tell you that I've already scheduled that faker for a mechanically assisted colon exam, there are bigger problems at

it. Did Holly bother to mention the attack on the Gulf

in passing. Why? What happened?" It confirms my low opinion
~~~~~ renshaw as I catch a slight nervousness in Stacy's tone.

"All of the clones in the six-pack were killed and the real José has been kidnapped by Apostle's people."

"That's awful! Why would they do that?"

"We suspect they are going to give him over to Doc Mangler for experimentation. José is more important than any poser. Besides, I was hoping that you would do the debunking for me, if ya don't mind? Any luck with the volcano girl?"

"I've located her. Had to drive off a group of folks who think they should sacrifice her."

"Can't you just evac her and be done with it?"

"No can do," she answers. "Anytime she strays more than fifteen kilometers from the mountain, the seismic activity starts up. It's a hostage crisis just waiting to happen! She's with one of the local heroes and a couple of government folks right now, and we're trying to work out a security arrangement moving forward. Long story short, if you are counting on me to handle this new Cal Stringel, you're going to be waiting for at least a week or more. Sorry!"

"Don't sweat it, beautiful," I say. "You should ask Holly to check the damn fake out and put her ass to work!"

Of course with my luck, the two of them would hit it off. That would be the ultimate middle finger from the universe.

"It's not a horrible idea," the Love Goddess says after a few seconds of mulling things over. "What are you doing?"

I sigh. "Watching Andy run the suit. He's helping the Gulf Coasters get their systems back online and as much as I hate to admit it, he's running the suit better than I can."

"That bothers you, doesn't it?" She hits the nail on the head.

"You have no idea, Stacy."

"You shouldn't let it. You rock that armor. Everything it can do is because of you."

"I know. I know."

One of my latest obsessions is peak efficiency. Every new metric I come up with, Andy beats me by easily fifteen percent and I'll be hanged if I know how to close the gap. I've built the most awesome blend of magic and tech, but other than taking it into combat, Andy runs rings around me. It is disappointing to say the least.

Deciding to change the topic, I bring her in on the other news of the day. "Also, Paper Tiger is in on our existence now. He agrees about the threat to José."

"Really?" she asks, clearly enjoying the tidbit of gossip. My trials and tribulations aside, this is gossip and it's important to her. "I was wondering how he and Wendy were moving forward. She finally took the next step!"

"I'm not so sure, Ms. Not-So-Hopeless Romantic. Bobby actually told him during their fight. If you ask me, Wendy doesn't look as happy as I thought she would when Tiger showed up. Anyway, don't be surprised if you're here and he suddenly walks in."

"Whenever I can get back there, you mean," she accuses. "That's what you're really getting at."

I roll the wooden cylinder and spot two more places where I can fit additional runes. "That too, but I know the drill. Maybe the two of us can schedule a rendezvous with our armor in some remote location if it doesn't look like you can break away. Worst case scenario, if we get seen, you could say that I'm the phony."

"That could actually work, but are you sure Mr. Hermit Crab is able to leave his shell? Are you sure you're not the imposter?"

It works as both teasing and innuendo, so I laugh. That's the thing people don't understand about Stacy. Under that incredible body she has lurks a very sarcastic soul. Our wit seems to line up in some kind of harmonic fashion. The only one I ever felt anything close to this with was Vicky, before she died. Vicky had been out of my league. Of course, Stacy is pretty much out of everyone's league, so if she has to be with someone, why the hell shouldn't it be me?

You won't catch me complaining!

Answering her, I say, "There's that, plus I want those in-person revelations that you have been stalling on. Why were you so freaked out when I bluffed and pretended to be an alien to the West Coast Losers back in Phoenix?"

"Yeah. That too."

"Stacy, our line is about as secure as it can get." Besides, I replaced that lie with another lie fairly quickly. The Big Lie is something of a specialty of mine. Done properly, it's a thing of beauty rivaling the woman I am talking to. Perhaps that's my real power?

"I'd still rather have this conversation face to face," she replies. "It's that important."

"I'm all for anything that gets you into my arms. You know that," I say, sensing that she's actually worried.

Something tells me I'm not gonna like what she has to say, but I will deal with it when the time comes.

"You're adorable, Cal! Duty calls. It looks like I'm needed. I'll see what I can do about putting Athena on the fake Cal's case. Let me know if you have anything on José Six-Pack. Don't do anything rash."

People keep saying that to me. Am I really that impulsive? "Will do, sweetness. Don't let a chunk of the Philippines blow up on your end. Your PR department would be disappointed in you."

Disconnecting, I look at the magical protection device and a piece of the dinosaur mage's teleportation mirror that it is supposed to insulate.

Imposters, volcanos, magic, kidnappings, secrets, and super science. Apparently those count as First World dating problems of the super-powered set. Hell! If it weren't for Stacy, I'd be sitting here obsessing over how I can compete with Andy when using my tech. Maybe those patches Bobby brought back from his fight with Seawall. He didn't say those guys were any faster, just stronger and semi-invincible. That won't work. Other drugs? Too risky. Hand/eye coordination training? I could practice on my drums more often, but even at the top of my game I'll still be slow compared to Andy.

My eyes go back to the mirror fragment and I look down under the bench where the silver plates I'd taken from Tyrannosorcerer Rex remained in stasis. *Magic helps run the suit. What if I magic up the suit operator? I was stronger and faster when I transformed into a human/lizard hybrid, and I've been doing all those exercises to strengthen the little magic I can access.*

Grabbing a beat-up spiral notebook, I flip through odds and ends for my various designs and locate the next blank sheet. I almost get distracted by a couple of nifty ideas that haven't made it off the pages yet. Forcing myself back on task, I look for my notes from my time trying to reverse Andy being turned to stone. Yeah, my Mark III armor got destroyed at that time, too, and I am absolutely not still bitter about that. To make the magic work, I had to try and become more cold-blooded to use dinosaur-based magic. After I succeeded in saving Andy's head, I'd left the reptilian lifestyle by the wayside and focused on the more accessible and simpler human spells. Making a broom sweep up a mess, making water bottles and milk jugs float, and the like. Augmented with the totem, I managed to make a mage bolt once.

Damn near passed out from the effort, but I am stronger now . . . OK, maybe not that much stronger.

Snatching up a pen, I begin to sketch. I start with the Gepetto suit I use to control Mega. Most of the tech is external and the ambient magic shouldn't interfere. I draw the totem containing Rex's talon-like claw onto a belt. The belt would need to be snake or gator to have the transformation runes inscribed. The entire suit might need to be for all I know. I'd need a hole on my backside for the tiny tail, but what do I care if anyone here sees my ass. It might need one or two more things to help augment my meager power, but I already knew that I'd have to go through with the design. Destiny calls my name and it cries out for something never seen before.

A human/dinosaur hybrid-operated suit of magical techno battle armor! Why has it taken over sixty-five million years to make this happen? Let's see some imposter dream up that shit! Stacy said not to do something rash. She didn't say not to do something dripping in awesomesauce!

Chapter Three

A Conflict of Biblical Proportions

Back in my villain days, I pretty much swore that the moment I committed a crime, there was someone, somewhere, already dispatching a smug dipshit of a hero to stop me.

My days as a Gulf Coast Guardian showed me how stupid that notion was. In between their paid appearances, promotional events, testimonials in front of Congress, and any number of other ego-stroking activities, the hero teams blunder around in the semi-dark and occasionally stumble onto a supervillain just trying to pull a job.

OK, maybe it's not that bad, but I've been on both sides of the fence, so my opinion counts for more than others' opinions—just ask me.

Either way, sit a week after one of my few hero friends' abduction, sifting through information that Andy's algorithms have fed me, looking for any clues where José might be and scoring a big fat nada. To say it is disheartening would be an understatement, but it's all I can do at the moment.

Frozen in Impotence, the true story of Calvin Matthew Stringel, I think, while sifting through another intercepted Interpol dispatch and waiting for the translation feature to do its thing. If I borrowed the necklace that tamps down Larry's power, I wouldn't need a translation engine, but Larry is still too scared to take it off.

The circumstances behind his several decades of insanity involved his obscene power levels and the death of his mother caused by those same obscene power levels. Back then, he retreated into the recesses of his mind because he couldn't cope. All of us have worked with him, trying to convince him that he's more mature, and better able to cope with his telekinesis. It hasn't exactly worked, but with repetition it might sink in.

I guess I'd be scared too if I had that kind of power, but I have reached the point where I am by being nothing more than a clever guy who also happens to be an asshole—or maybe just an asshole who also happens to be clever. It is kind of tough to decide which one comes first. Opinions vary.

Not seeing anything useful in the translated dispatch, I close it and bring up the latest footage of the sphincter pus that is impersonating me holding a press conference.

"Mr. Stringel? Mr. Stringel? Are you planning to rebuild your armor and rejoin the Gulf Coast Guardians?"

"I do plan to get back into a suit of armor, but I'm going to do it on my own terms. First, I'm waiting to see what kind of back pay I'll be getting from them and clearing up all my other financial issues relating to my return. Once I have a good handle on how much I have to work with, that'll determine whether I just go with a version of the Mark Three or if I can start designing a Mark Four. But more important than that, I need to try and see my baby girl."

"So you're saying that you're prioritizing your daughter over being a superhero?"

Fake Cal has clearly mastered my "I'm surprised you can breathe and be that stupid" look.

"What do you think, idiot? Did you even read my autobiography? I signed on for a paycheck and a pardon. It took my almost dying to get that pardon they kept dangling over my head. Now I've got it and I'm missing all that money from when I got sent forward in time. I need to get things straight with my publisher to start getting my book earnings, especially now that I'm back on the bestseller lists. After all that's been settled, then yeah, I might consider returning to active duty with one of the Guardian teams. Next question."

"If I could follow up," the reporter comments.

"No!" the version of me onstage says. "You've already had your chance to be a moron. How about we give someone else a chance to lower the room's IQ? You, over there! Dazzle me!"

Sadly, it sounds like some of the things I would say. A clone is becoming more likely, but the question is how they replicated my thought patterns.

The next reporter took her time, appearing to carefully choose her words. "Mr. Stringel, I'm still a little unclear about how you were teleported almost two years into the future. Could you share a little more about how that happened?"

There's my eye roll and a deep breath. "OK, this one's for the people that will be leaving this event on the short bus. I invent things, in case that's escaped your notice. In this case, it was a prototype of an emergency teleportation device. You know, a way to get out of my armor in a hurry, like maybe when I'm holding an overheating nuclear core that's about to go. Seems like it worked, but the only thing I can think of is that it absorbed some of the power that core was throwing out and that caused the rift I opened . . . Shit! I can already see I'm wasting my breath on most of you. Let me put it this way: The prototype got a big push from the reactor and I got a chance to call myself a time traveler. If you want more detail, we can do that, and it's going to cost you. Also, you better get ready for all the people watching this to tune out."

"But shouldn't the radiation have killed you?"

"If I didn't have all that shielding and an experimental teleportation unit powering up, yeah, it should have. I'm lucky to be alive. Damn lucky! And you can bet your ass I'm going to be on a first-name basis with my oncologist, who will be screening me for cancer every damn month! Next stupid question."

Despite my natural anger, I must confess I am enjoying this. The imposter is maybe a little too smooth with his answers and his insults are playing to the crowd. The reality of me in front of the press would involve more stuttering and stammering than this well-rehearsed indignation. The fact that Megan Bostic is standing on the stage along with him makes me see a conspiracy.

Then again, Megan is the very definition of an opportunist and my suddenly being alive must be very good for her business. Don't get me wrong; Megan and I had some good times when we were putting my book together. She's as jaded as I am when it comes to heroes, maybe more. As bad as Patterson screwed me over, he literally screwed her over and then left her.

I ponder her bitterness as a reflection of my own as I watch the fake handle additional questions and I search for the chinks in the imposter's armor. Categorizing his answers, I judge how I would have answered the same questions. At least knowing the background of who the imposter is interacting with will help me when I finally decide to confront the person, or the clone, who stole my life.

Odds are, their defense would be that I wasn't really using it anyway. I do confess to being curious about the denials the fraud will try. It might be the only thing that keeps them alive for very long.

I asked Andy to make sure that he's recording all of this so we can build a database on the imposter. After all, how often do you get the opportunity to psychoanalyze yourself?

At least Stacy will be home from her extended Pacific Rim Adventure this week and I will finally get the opportunity to hold her in my arms again, unless her jackass friends stumble into some other world-threatening plot. She has been gone for far too long for my liking. After all, I don't really care if Mount Pinatubo blows its top and destroys a few towns; it is interfering with my love life. Somehow, I don't think Stacy would see that the same way.

I suppose if she feels like I do, then she wouldn't be the person that I am in love with. Just because she makes me consider the possibility of being a better man doesn't mean that I want to drag my Olympian girlfriend down to my level. She has the entire world depending on her. Me? I can barely shoulder the responsibility of being on an illegal super team and chipping in to raise my daughter.

"I'm not getting anywhere with this," I say, realizing how far off track my mind has wandered. José isn't getting found anytime in the next few hours, at least not by me. All those folks who cry out that they won't rest until someone is rescued or saved—well, they're idiots. I function better on a good night's sleep.

"I will continue to search for potential leads on the Internet. Perhaps Mr. Walton will have better results on VillainNet? It is less than optimum, but I have provided him with several query strings he can attempt."

Cringing at the thought of Bobby attempting to find anything other than porn online, I do my best to nod at my favorite non-human. I constantly fight the temptation to turn Andy loose on the criminal version of the World Wide Web, but the Wireless Wizard would catch us and cut us off before we got anything useful. The Wizard has a special relationship with telecommunications. Running the hidden version of the criminal version of the Internet is more profitable than pulling bank jobs. Plus, the last time Wizard was in the public eye, he was huge. Who knows what he looks like now? He might have gone on a serious diet or have found a way to upload himself.

"What's Mega doing right now?" I ask Andy, jealous of his ability to multitask.

"We are out over the Pacific, responding to a fishing vessel in distress," he answers.

My mechanical brother from another circuit board doesn't mind doing the grunt work of the hero world. I'm sure the folks on that ship appreciate his diligence.

"Any systems showing wear and tear?"

"All of the systems are showing varying degrees, but there is not anything worth noting at this time."

Smartass, I think. Andy is kind of like the ultimate straight man. "We may need to schedule a maintenance window, soon. That's all for me. I'm going to get some sleep."

"Good night, Calvin."

Bobby is up in central command playing a game amidst a pile of beer cans as I finish climbing the steps.

"Thought you were already asleep," he says. "Burning the midnight oil?"

"Looking for the Six Pack. Seen any jobs south of the border?"

"Not really," he mutters. "Probably all those damn Manglermals down there taking up the jobs."

"There's a joke there, but I'm not going to make it. How about Eddie? Has his dumb ass shown up yet? I would love to beat some information out of him."

"Not a word from him, but he'll turn up sooner or later, kind of like herpes."

My response is interrupted by a door sliding open and a crying child. "Oh good, you're still up."

"I was about to turn in," I say to Wendy. "But I can sit up with her. Night terrors again?"

Doesn't look like sleep is coming any time soon.

Gabby has two of the most powerful supers for parents, but she still has the same problems that every kid experiences. Will she develop powers of her own? Do I even want her to get mixed up in this business?

Wendy passes Gabby off to me and turns back to her room, leaving me with an upset toddler in pink ducky pajamas.

"Rough night, huh kiddo? Let's go to my room and I'll put a Disney movie on. How about we go old school with *The Jungle Book*?"

• • •

Just outside the smog cloud that envelopes Mexico City, I meet up with Paper Tiger, our newest member—sort of. I'm still smarting from having to fly close to the ground after a couple of Mexican fighter jets began shadowing me. Who knew they gave a shit about their airspace?

Maybe I'll fly high on the way back if I'm in the mood to screw with them.

"Hello, Charles," I say as he exits the SUV. As strange as it is to see a Bengal tiger/human hybrid carrying a pair of taser batons at his side and a plasma pistol in a holster, it probably is the second strangest thing I have seen in the last hour, and it probably will not make the weekly top one hundred. "I see you've lost the Siberian look."

"I draw the fur heavier on the Siberians. It's too damn hot to be running around like that."

He's practical. I'll give him that. "What kind of leads did K-Otica have? Our mutual friend says most of the jobs down here are being taken by Manglermals."

I detect the approach of an airborne vehicle. Small profile, one hundred fourteen miles per hour, two passengers, hoversled, two hundred thirty-seven feet above ground level. IFF code Gulf Coast Guardians.

"You were followed," I say to Phipps and gesture to the sky. I'm not really in the mood to deal with those K-Otica and Spiritstaff today, but there is the old saying from Mick Jagger about not always getting what you want.

"Should have known when they lent me the vehicle."

"Yes, you should have," I say. Neither one of us is truly there. Phipps is in his little private sanctum, supposedly in Nevada based on my best guess, and I am, of course, in the control chair in Alabama, but it is somewhat irritating that we are being followed.

Amateur hour at its worst. Wendy will probably give me no end of shit over it, but the upside is that she will have to chew out her boyfriend as well.

Popping the visor up on my immersion helmet, I beckon to Andy and shut off the external microphone. "Andy, better take over the conversation. I don't care for Spiritstaff, and the last time I had any real conversation with Karina, she was my hostage."

Ah, the good old days . . .

Andy cuts over onto the command circuit and I reluctantly relinquish control to him.

The hoversled descends and the former Gulf Coasters climb off. Karina is in a darker costume than the bright swirling colors she used to wear. Perhaps an attempt at being somewhat stealthy, completely ruined by her long pink hair. If Karina is going to be a walking billboard for loud fashion statements, she should just own the look.

Considering I would have said that to her, tagging Andy in remains a good idea.

Her husband, Mystigal's brother, irritates me. His magic staff blocks anything that comes his way—up to a point. Beyond that, he's a world-class martial artist. One of my fondest memories from my villain days is seeing the look on his face when I tossed a dumpster at him. Of course his Latina wife went into a berserker rage at that and wiped the asphalt with Hillbilly Bobby, and I'd been lucky to get out of there with my Mark II Cal suit still functioning. Bobby took a trip to the hospital and then to prison.

Karina's power levels fluctuate on an hourly basis. At her peak, she is a top-tier threat—flying, energy beams, and an adrenaline-enhanced temper. On her off hours, she's a little bitchy, can run and jump faster and higher than normal humans, and makes a pretty light show that is more amusing than threatening.

"Greetings," Andy offers.

"So this is the vaunted Megasuit?" K-Otica says in Spanish. I glance at the scanners to see if I can get a read on her power levels. My best guess is that she's near her peak and that makes her more confrontational—almost a 'roid rage situation. "I'm surprised you are working with it, Tiger."

"He considers José a friend as well," Charles replies. "He also appreciates the gravity of the situation if Doctor Mangler is experimenting on José. As you can see, I have all the backup I need. You two don't have to tag along."

Paper Tiger also appears to be annoyed at being followed.

"It is good to see you, Andydroid. I can't remember the last time we worked together," Spiritstaff says.

It's a test. One that I would have failed.

"It was when we took the Silver Squad into custody in Macon, Georgia. Six hundred forty-one days ago."

Back in the base, I laugh and tell Andy that he should have given the value in seconds just to screw with him.

"Longer than I'd thought," Spiritstaff says. "You've changed."

"There is a human expression that change is constant. I still find it odd that your species creates statements that are contradictory on purpose. But you are indeed correct that much has changed. You and Karina have married and procreated. The human race was almost exterminated by an ill-conceived genetic experiment. I have been disassembled and turned to stone, crafted a more useful body using Calvin Stringel as an inspiration, and made a decision to protect humanity from its own self-destructive tendencies. Your skin pigmentation is seventeen percent darker. Are you enjoying the warmer climate of Mexico?"

Come to think of it, Andy is actually pretty good at messing with people.

Spiritstaff holds up a finger. "I am enjoying my wife's homeland, but I can say that not all change is for the better. You have also fought against my sister and her team."

"They picked a fight with my team," Andy corrects. "They chose poorly."

"True, but you have also shown that you are willing to take a human life," he says, unconcerned by Andy's interruption.

"Ultraweapon's actions in San Francisco killed dozens and injured hundreds. His armor constituted a weapon of mass destruction. My actions were justified to remove him as a threat so that his nuclear-powered warbot and the other warbots could be stopped."

I make a note to ask Andy if he truly believes that. He's justifying what I did to Lazarus Patterson, and doing a better job of it than I ever could have. It makes me consider if Andydroid actually believes what he is saying.

Spiritstaff scratches his chin. "Even so, we shall come with you and observe your behavior, old friend. Showing restraint on this day would be a way of demonstrating that you have not degenerated into an amoral killing machine."

Andy actually does pause at that for two whole seconds.

"We are coming and that is not negotiable," Karina states and adjusts her pistol belt. She's packing a pair of bioshockers for those times of the day when she's not feeling so fresh. "Our lead is in the jungles approximately two hours south of here. There is an encampment of Manglermals that appears to be some form of training base or a recruiting center. Our source indicated between forty and fifty Manglers present. The leader is presumed to be White Rhino, a mercenary for hire currently wanted by Interpol for numerous crimes in Africa."

"I find this arrangement agreeable. I will do my best to ensure your safety, but the overriding objective is to learn the whereabouts of Doctor Mangler. There is a low probability of damage to this suit based on the capabilities of a typical Manglermal. I will take point and suppress their electronic communications. The three of you will prevent any of the Manglers from escaping. Optionally, we could employ Paper Tiger as an inside agent before resorting to hostilities. His form could be construed as a Manglermal. This course of action carries a slightly increased risk for Mr. Phipps, but significantly decreases the potential for collateral damage."

Karina holds up her finger and says, "Even though Charles could have his current form destroyed and not really suffer, I think that we can go ahead with the first option. White Rhino is a wanted criminal and we have the opportunity to question him while we bring him to the authorities."

Charles takes that moment to comment that whenever one of his drawings is destroyed, it gives him a terrible headache. While he is doing that, I wonder what is with Karina and her husband and holding up their fingers. Home life with these two must be strange. There are probably several jokes I could make, but I am stuck in a position where I can't make a single one of them!

The struggles of a sarcastic asshole. The fight is real!

The group settles down for a quick discussion about the logistics. Spiritstaff flies back to get the picture frame Phipps uses to travel here since they have only one hoversled. He can climb back into the frame and they can carry it in the sled's cargo compartment. It is somewhat refreshing. If they were still working for the U.S. government, there would be red tape without end to work through to coordinate this with the Mexican officials. Instead, Karina calls the personal cellphone of the Attorney General and politely informs the man about our plans.

It's nice to have people around me that have some decent pull. It's a definite upgrade from the way my things usually end up.

On second thought, I probably shouldn't jinx myself.

• • •

For anyone considering the glamourous life of a jungle mercenary, I should take a picture of the ramshackle collection of battered trailers, trucks, and tents. It looks . . . quaint. With amenities like an open latrine trench and the stack of rusted fifty-five-gallon drums, it's surprising that more people don't come here.

The welcoming committee shows up in the form of a hastily fired shoulder-launched stinger missile—good old American technology and yet another instance of Uncle Sam being a tad careless with his toys. In the old days, I made a living off government idiocy. I've mellowed, and these days it just irritates me.

"Going loud," I transmit to the three heroes assisting me.

One of the nice things about fighting humanoids that have undergone a partial animal transformation is that many of them have a heightened sense of hearing. I give them the Biloxi Bugler treatment and observe the chaos. The missile shooter, some kind of leopard or jaguar, collapses on the ground as my high-pitched wail tortures it.

"Bad kitty!" I mutter and descend. The suit comes in hot, with automatic weapon fire plinking off my shields like rain on a car's windshield.

Shutting off the sonics, I see Manglerals stumbling around. It brings a smile to my face.

This should be an easy cleanup, I think before I can stop myself.

"Missile inbound." I hear the same voice from my suit that warned me about the stinger thirty seconds ago. It belongs to a dead woman, the first real love of my life, Vicky. Despite my flourishing relationship with Stacy,

I haven't parted with the last few audio files Vicky recorded before she went up in the explosion that destroyed Omega Base.

I expect the missile to be an RPG-7. The Russians are even more careless with their tinker toys than Uncle Sam is.

And then I get a scan on it. Shit! It's an overloaded powercell missile. Just like I used against Patterson's first atomic robot! Bastards must have read my book! I think this is the first time other than being shot with force blasters that someone has turned one of my inventions on me!

I don't like it one bit!

The improvised weapon detonates on my front shields and it takes a good thirty percent off the top.

"Missile inbound. Missile inbound. Missile inbound." I get to hear Vicky again. These are actual RPG-7s. Guess they didn't have too many powercells to spare. Good thing, too!

"Increasing power to the forward shield generators," Andy says from his console as my plasma cannons try to run interference. Two of the three hammer on my weakened shields and Mega actually staggers. The blasts barely scrape the paint job, but even so, it rattles me. I don't like being rattled.

"Shields at sixty percent." Andy provides a dismal update. "Recommend we swap out the two of the four forward shield modules."

"We can do it as soon as you tell me what the hell is shooting us." *Cakewalks aren't supposed to be like this.*

"A speedster," Andy answers as two more RPGs are fired at me. The small arms fire stops as the Manglermals sprint for the jungle. Memories of Maxine Velocity, using my weapon designs, running circles around Ultraweapon before he killed her, assault me. I am on the other side of the equation this time.

"I hate speedsters! Andy, warn the rest that there's a little more waiting here than a trip to the zoo. Have them circle the base and see if they can get some of the runners."

"I am informing your three allies on scene. Larry, Wendy, and Bobby are being notified as well."

"Energy spike detected." The warning is in Andy's voice. Vicky never got to that one.

A bolt of energy smashes into my shields. It is similar to my sparring sessions with Larry Hitt.

Threat assessment locks onto the source of the psychic battering ram, a thin man floating in the air next to a broken-down Chevy truck. His limbs dangle uselessly as another bolt of white energy is launched at me.

Jorge Delgado—The Holy Ghost. One of the Apostle's Faithful. He's a heavy duty telekinetic with Lou Gehrig's disease. That means the speedster is probably The Grace of the Almighty—a terminal brain cancer patient named Mitch Calhoun. His top speed is around two hundred seventy-five miles per hour.

I've fought faster with much less than Mega and won. Maybe it's arrogance, or maybe I am really pissed about José, but I start the suit forward and cut loose with the sonics again. The weapons panel shows green and I cycle through the cannons and lay down a barrage of plasma bolts for suppressing fire. The Faithful are zealots, all dying of fatal conditions and kept alive by Apostle's transferred power. They'd most definitely know where my friend is, but the odds of their giving up that nugget of information without a telepath are slim and none.

Apostle has committed two of his six followers to this ambush. But are the rest ready to pop out of the woodwork? The whole group together might pose a serious threat.

There's a rush of air through the room and I hear the boots of my boss hit the floor behind me. Here comes the cavalry.

"Larry's suited up. He'll be here in a second. I need you to pull back so that we can deploy without the others noticing."

"Where's Gabby?" I'm cool enough in the situation to ask about our baby girl.

"Bobby," she says, sounding disgusted at her own choice of emergency child care. Alone with a kitchen drawer full of knives might be a better option.

"Andy's trying to convince K-Otica and Spiritstaff to fall back. We're obviously expected," I say to Whirlwendy. "I can take 'em. They've got to have all kinds of surveillance on the area. We shouldn't use the poop shoot."

Wendy grumbles for a minute. "I can climb into the suit and you can pop the seal. I'll come out like I've always been there and bring up a storm to cover you deploying Larry."

I want to argue, but it's an argument I'll lose. I did after all ask her to lead the team.

"Switching off the sonics. Climb on in, Wendy. I'll take Mega up."

"No, stay on the ground. Let's show them what kind of tricks we have up our sleeves."

It's my turn to grumble. I don't like unbuttoning the suit in the middle of combat, even with my shields up. Weapon fault light on plasma cannon three. I flip the toggle and the overheating plasma cannon slides back from the mirror fragment and is replaced by a twenty-millimeter chain gun. The rhythmic thumping of the weapon's recoil begins as I send enough depleted uranium rounds toward the Holy Ghost that he's forced to pull a big rock in front of him to shield him from my firepower.

"I'm keeping Holy Ghost pinned down, boss! Too many targets to track with the speedster. Better come out at full force."

"Right," she replies. "I'm in position. Count it down, Cal."

"Missile inbound. Missile inbound." OK, I like Vicky's voice, but this is getting ridiculous.

"Hang on. Two more RPGs on my rear quadrant. Let my shields take them first."

The shields register the impacts. I nod to Andy and he saves me the trouble of typing the commands with the keyboard. "Unzipping in seven, six, five, four, three, two, one, go, go, go!"

The pressure inside the suit drops as the chest plate falls open. Wendy's arms emerge and a wave of air pressure spreads out in my forward arc as the wind speed rises.

Wendy leaps out and shoots vertical as my chest piece begins moving back into place. High-speed dust particles moving inside the suit could easily be more damaging than the RPGs and telekinetic bolts. I use her cover to rotate one of the depleted shield modules out.

She doesn't waste time on lame superhero monologues. Hell, no one would hear her anyway! Her air vortex surrounds us and the next RPG is blown off course. At two on one odds, Grace and Holy Ghost could pester me even if they weren't really doing much damage.

With her arrival, shit just got real for them. The tiny tornado maker with one of the foulest mouths ever to speak the English language taps into Mother Nature and suddenly the little camp is less of a warzone and more of a disaster area.

Under the cover of Wendy's tornado, I flip the large crystal fragment around and point to Larry Hitt—Big Red. "Show that sonnuvabitch Delgado what real power is."

Larry nods and I give him the thumbs-up.

Seconds later, my scanners are swamped with the twenty-foot-tall energy construct manifesting in the center of our private little storm. Larry's energy beast walks through the eyewall of the tornado as if it were a gentle breeze.

If Holy Ghost didn't crap his pants when Wendy arrived, this probably pushed him over the edge. Andy swaps out the other shield module with a fresh one and I'm back to full strength.

I see bolts of energy thrown like spears from Delgado like some ancient Greek warrior trying to bring down a cyclops. Larry shrugs them off like bee stings as his arms stretch out try to catch Holy Ghost in his giant energy hands. It's only a matter of time.

"Larry's got this," I say to Andy. "Where's Grace?"

"Ninety-three percent chance he is fleeing. There is too much interference to accurately determine."

I didn't like it. Apostle isn't that attached to his Faithful and is more than willing to sacrifice them. His "blessing" weakens over the course of seven days until it disappears completely—very biblical and all that happy horseshit, but Apostle could always find new replacements. Rumor is that he had a waiting list. Some wanted to live, others wanted revenge, and the rest probably just wanted to score a big payday before their death.

My concerns become a reality as The Grace of the Almighty returns, knifing through the buffeting winds with some kind of high-yield suicide vest strapped to him, aiming for the side of Big Red. Wendy rockets high and away on instinct and Larry barely has time to process what Andy is saying before the speedster disintegrates in a ball of flames, toppling my friend. Delgado wastes no time and attacks Larry like a man possessed. My friend's energy form does the equivalent of a fetal ball to protect him.

I use my jetpack and leapfrog over Larry, coming down between him and Holy Ghost. I see the crazed look in the man's eyes. He doesn't care whether he lives or dies.

Funny thing is, I don't care whether he does either. My chaingun starts up again, and I bracket him with all three plasma cannons. Then I unleash my own personal Armageddon on him.

His attacks on Larry stop and within a few seconds, this incarnation of The Holy Ghost receives his ticket to the afterlife.

I probably won't score any points with the other heroes who came here wanting to "observe" Megasuit, but the world needs people like Larry Hitt and Wendy LaGuardia to save it . . .

And they need someone like me to do what's necessary to make sure they are around to be the real heroes.

I can live with that.

Chapter Four

Awful Truths Disguised as Pillow Talk

In the cleanup from the mess that was our little Mexican adventure, we didn't learn very much. Karina and her husband, along with Paper Tiger, captured nine Manglermals. They were all low-level foot soldiers and whatever leads they offered were not worth spending any time on. White Rhino had been out of the camp when it was attacked. The consensus was that General Devious and the Apostle had set a trap to see who was going to come looking for José Six Pack.

Andy is still checking through what little electronic salvage we recovered from the site. Unfortunately, the explosions, tornado, and the plasma discharges did not leave too much that could be forensically analyzed.

Unfortunately, we don't really do subtle, even by the loosest definition of the word.

Even though we are fresh out of leads on José for the moment, I am in an upbeat mood. Stacy is almost here. Sure, the imposter is out on the talk show circuit and sucking up to the public in general. I'll give credit where it's due, the fake's story is staying consistent. He even passed the genetic test Athena gave him, meaning he's a clone or a really good shapeshifter. To me it smells like the Overlord's handiwork. Our last encounter with me pulling off the Andydroid ruse left me realizing that the Archvillain would use unconventional tactics coming after us.

That reminds me, I need to come up with a defense for overcharged power cell. It still burns my ass that they used one of my ideas and used it against me.

Still, the world can piss off for a day. Stacy is on her way here. I've been a good little boy and only a few people died. I deserve a break. OK, maybe that's a bad example. Fine, I've been a bad little boy and I deserve a spanking. Whichever way she wants to go, I'm covered.

"Andy? Did the Flora finish cleaning up my room?" I ask, hissing a little. The dinoform has boosted my performance by a whopping eight percent on average. I'm still not close to Andy's statistics, but I'm getting as close as humanly, or perhaps inhumanly, possible.

"Yes, she did," Andy answers.

"Thanks, pal. I appreciate it." I wonder if I should design a second set of controls for when I'm transformed.

"You should thank her," Andy answers. "She was the one that performed the task."

"Oh, you're right," I say, playing along. I bring up our base chat application and click on Flora's name. The woman's face appears. "Thanks for taking care of my room and making dinner for when Stacy gets here."

"No problem, dear. You two are absolutely adorable together. I left a dress shirt and a pair of slacks out for you. I think Stacy would appreciate it if you dressed up for her."

Flora is really just a modified Type-A robot with a full cosmetic skin job. She and her "husband" James are Andy's attempt at portraying a "normal" couple, who are renovating the property above our base and converting it into a bed and breakfast. Our only saving grace is that the locals know that Flora and James are from California; that seems to excuse their odd behavior.

Andy is programming them to be human, which is amusing because Andydroid might be an excellent observer of the human condition, but he isn't the best at actually applying it—like anyone actually is, but give him credit for trying.

As a result, Flora enjoys interacting with me and tries to act like a big sister to me. James doesn't like me at all and thinks I'm an ass. I'm fairly certain Andy is screwing with me, so at least I am keeping my friend entertained. They are our cover, our topside security, and can probably handle a SWAT unit, but not much more than that. We don't really count them as part of the team.

Neither of them likes Bobby, but that's not a surprise since Andy shares the same opinion of my other friend.

Maybe Andy is becoming more human than he realizes. I can't really point fingers given that, depending on which day it is, I am either trying to turn myself into a dinosaur/human hybrid or looking for new ways to fully integrate myself into Megasuit.

"When is Aphrodite arriving?" Wendy strolls down the stairs with our tiny poop producer in her arms. She never refers to my girlfriend as Stacy. Bobby thinks it's a jealousy thing. Me? I can't see Wendy acting the least bit attracted to me, even after I recruited her and my girlfriend wasn't in the picture at all. So I'm in the camp of Wendy being slightly intimidated by Stacy's presence and being extra angry when the Olympian is around.

"T-minus two hours until Cal becomes less cranky," I reply.

"At least you didn't lie and say that you'd be friendlier, but since you're talking about yourself in third person, I think you need some human company. Until she gets here, mind dropping the whole lizard act and watching Gabrielle?"

"Let me disconnect and turnover to Andy. What's the weather like topside?"

"It's Alabama in late summer. Take a damn guess. But if you're going to take her up for some fresh air, I can probably arrange a cool breeze. Both of you could use some sun."

I don't need to be a meteorologist to forecast that it will be mostly bitchy down here if I don't let Wendy have some alone time.

Feeling Andy jack into Mega, I unhook and say, "I had it. You got it."

Not exactly a thorough turnover, but Andy will be on top of things within five seconds—probably less. And no, I'm not jealous one bit. Concentrating for a second, I feel the tail and claws begin to disappear as my body reverts to normal Cal Stringel. Stacy doesn't know about my use of performance-enhancing magic yet. I figure I should try and surprise her.

"That really fucking creeps me out," Wendy says as I slip out of the lizard version of my control suit and hang it up next to the human version. Being naked in front of Wendy doesn't bug me in the least, but I slide on a pair of boxers and then some shorts. My T-shirt says World's Best Dinosaur Magic User.

Nothing but the truth from me.

• • •

"Da," Gabby says with pride and points at me. Talking is a new thing for her. Naturally, "Mama" came first, but given all the curse words that project from Wendy's mouth on a regular basis, I am shocked Gabby's first words didn't have to be censored.

Her black hair is in little pigtails. Wendy did them. My attempts are not nearly that symmetrical and apparently, that matters. But when Gabby's hair is long enough for a ponytail, Wendy is in trouble. I have a programmable actuator and patterns that'll do all kind of crazy things.

Ruined a few wigs at first, but it hasn't scalped a mannequin in three weeks. It should be kid-safe and mother-approved in another eight weeks.

The breeze is nice. Having a weather manipulator running the team has benefits. I'm wearing a Crimson Tide ball cap and big sunglasses. Andy checks the satellite movements periodically, but there is always the likelihood that somebody has one up there that we don't know about. Of course, there's an imposter running around in California, so maybe it is just paranoia, which is my usual state. It reminds me that if I can ever reverse engineer the mirrors, we can find a way to move the base to Mars and be completely untouchable.

I walk with Gabby in my arms around the pond. The level is still low from Megasuit's firefighting adventures. Wendy steers storms into our area, but has to be careful that it isn't too noticeable. Suffice to say Farmer's Almanac is a little off this season.

Inside of the workshop, I could see James working on our next defensive upgrade. A regular horse would struggle under the weight of a Type-A robot, so naturally the solution is to build a robot horse, right around the frame of a pulse cannon. We have a handful of Type B's, but it's easier to hide a fake horse on a bed and breakfast with the fake people. The downside is that with all of us pretty much hiding from the law, our stores of spare parts are running low.

In the old days, I'd be searching the Internet for factories to knock over. This new lifestyle has me in the technological equivalent of blue balls.

My daughter interrupts my pity party. "Owyn." This translates to her wanting down.

I grant her request and hold her arm so she can stagger around like a little drunken sailor. A little of the old fatherly pride appears. The colossal screwups in my life are longer than a line at the DMV on the last day of the month, but the little babbling hellion getting her exploring on is the one screwup that makes all those others worthwhile.

It's something I'm actually good at.
Maybe the only thing that doesn't involve killing.
I wonder if Stacy would want . . .
Better not finish that thought.
Maybe I should talk to her first.
Ease it into the conversation and feel her out on it.
Probably wouldn't go for it just yet.
The press would hound her endlessly about who the father is.
She wouldn't anyway.
But she says she loves me.

• • •

Instead of a hoversled, a nondescript black van pulls up in the driveway. James walks out to meet the driver and waves her on through after a second. I ease myself off the swing where I've been rocking the now-sleeping daughter. I feel like I'm carrying an extra five pounds of drool.

Reaching the van just as it finishes backing up to the garage, I see Stacy smiling at me. She climbs out wearing a Redskins ball cap, a T-shirt, and shorts that look comfortable but still show a generous amount of leg.

"Hey, you," she says with a whisper. "I brought her some clothes and a couple of toys."

"Thanks. What happened? Lose your pilot's license?" I tease. Technically, no one ever gets a license for hoversleds. Hell, I even flew them a couple of times . . . rather poorly, too. As far as I am concerned, hoversleds are for chumps who don't want to learn how to use a jet pack.

"Brought my armor along, Cal. I figured it was time to let you make good on those mods you keep mentioning."

I'm stunned. "You brought your armor for me to upgrade? How long are you staying?"

"At least two weeks. Think you can complete the maintenance by then?"

"Yeah, I think I can," I reply.

She smiles. "Well, make sure you reserve some play time. I like free labor and all that jazz, but I did come here to see you, loverboy."

"I'd offer to hand you Gabby and take your luggage, but we both know you're stronger than I am. Larry's in town. I'll ask him to float your armor down the elevator when he gets back." The truth doesn't really hurt in this case. So she's stronger than I am. So what?

"You look like Christmas has come early," she states while wagging a suggestive finger at me.

"You're here, and you brought tech. Way better than a fat guy in a red suit."

Stacy hefts her suitcases with ease and follows me to the elevator. Her aura perks people up and Gabby is no exception. By the time we finish our descent, my daughter is wide awake and trying to coax my girlfriend into taking her. Her Aphrodite aura can affect kids and make them hyperactive.

It has other effects on males, I'm happy to say.

Only five minutes are required for Stacy to greet everyone here while I hand Gabby off to Wendy. I offer the lame excuse of having to help her unpack, which is a euphemism. At some point later, her suitcases will be unpacked, but now is not that time. As soon as the door to my suite shuts, I'm on her like a hormonal teenager.

"Missed you," I mutter between kisses. "Nice tan."

"You cleaned," she observes and slides her lips across my neck.

"Flora helped." I see no reason to hide the truth. Stacy brings out the best in me. "She's also making us dinner."

"Your team is so delightfully strange, Cal. You know that?"

I can only nod because I really don't want to have any deep discussions right now. I just want her, and my only plans at the moment involve showing her how much I have missed her for the next hour or so. Excluding the period where she thought I was dead, this has been our longest separation to date.

• • •

OK, so maybe I didn't manage to last as long as I usually do, but she hit her second-level thing, so I feel my efforts weren't wasted; points scored by all. Right now, I am snuggled in close with an arm around her body. We're playing the talking game since most any other game would probably involve the Cal-falls-asleep game.

Stacy sighs and says, "We should get up soon. Bitch gotta eat, if you know what I mean?"

"You have a terrible potty mouth. The things I put up with."

She runs a finger through my hair. "You cut your hair really short. Any particular reason?"

"Testing out my robohairstylist. It needs more work."

A lot more work!

"Do you have any good news about Larry's kids?"

Stacy frowns. "Hermes is still on it. She was out following leads when I checked in. I feel bad for her because Holly told me she's a bit infatuated with a certain Mysterious Highwayman. I don't want to be there when she finds out that her Highwayman is really Bobby in disguise."

It's worth a chuckle. The female avatar of Hermes with the hots for Bobby. Actually, anyone with the hots for him is kind of funny. Then again, here I am in love with the most beautiful woman in the world. Stranger things have certainly happened. "Should we tell Bobby about it? Maybe in the future we can double date."

With a look of mock terror on her face, she answers, "Oh, hell no!"

"So are you glad to be back?"

"No, I'd rather be anywhere else but here right now." Stacy is turned away from me, so I can't see her roll her eyes, but I can practically hear them.

"Sarcastic wench."

"But you adore me anyway," she says.

"More than adore you," I answer. It's probably the afterglow of really good sex, but my decision to ease into a discussion about the future just disappears. "I'd marry you in a heartbeat. With that fake around, it would be interesting."

She shifts a little in my arms. "What're you saying?"

"I thought it was pretty obvious. I'm saying if we have to end this little ruse of me being dead because of that damn fake, I want to do it right."

"What does doing it right mean?"

She seems to have a lot of questions right now and my concern begins to grow. Still, I've come this far, so there's no turning back. "It means marriage and kids if you're up for it."

Her expression is a mixture of delight and something else that I can't immediately place.

"Damn," Stacy says after what seems like an eternity.

That isn't something I want to hear after exposing my emotions like that.

"What's wrong?" I ask. "I'm actually good with kids. It's not your image. I know you too well for it to be that."

"Remember my empathic abilities," she says.

"Yeah, you can tell what people want if you focus. That should tell you how much I want this."

"And you really want more kids," she states with a certain finality.

"You don't want any?"

"Want? Sure. Am able to? Not right now. Check back in a few hundred years."

"Wait! What?"

"It's an ugly truth the twelve of us don't talk about. When the Olympians transferred their power to us, it reset us inside. My body is essentially a toddler inside. Our life expectancy is thousands of years. I won't really be fertile for maybe six hundred years at the earliest."

"Oh." It's all I can say at the moment.

"Now you know why I wanted to tell you in person. This isn't just a casual kind of chat I wanted to have over the comm channel."

"I think I am starting to see why. How deep does the rabbit hole go?"

"Sweetheart, we have only just started. Buckle up, honey, and say the word when you've had enough. Remember all those Greek myths where they did all those horrible things to men and women?"

"Yeah. Let me guess, the terrible twos?"

"Close, teenage years and puberty. Plus most of the originals were a bunch of asshats, super-powered asshats, even Aphrodite. She'd mellowed by the time I met her. But if you're wanting kids, you've got the wrong girl."

"So you won't even be able to . . ."

"No," her voice drops to a whisper. "One of the things the originals tried to drill into our heads was that everything we hold dear right now, we will outlive, and it will hurt like hell."

"Yeah, that would suck."

"It gets worse. When I can have kids, if I do it with someone who isn't an Olympian, I'll outlive my kids, too. All those Greek demigods? Most, if not all, of them existed. They have longer lifespans than regular humans, but only a few hundred years. The child of two Olympians might make it to five hundred unless the power of the Titans is transferred to them, then they get reset as well. This is what I have been holding back from you all this time."

I guess on some level I already know this, but it is still a shock. I am more than a little confused.

"I thought what you were holding back had to do with aliens, not the Olympians."

"Where do you think the Titans came from?" she asks.

"I don't know." But I suddenly have a bad feeling.

"The Titans were aliens. More specifically, deposed alien tyrants who had fled to Earth and decided to begin rebuilding here. They intended to make a new army and go back out into space and retake their empire from the Rigellians."

I don't care for the picture Stacy is painting. "Really?"

"Afraid so," she continues. "Anyway, their first experiments created the gods of Egypt, super-evolved animals and human hybrids. The Titans perfected the process and began creating enhanced humans—basically, the gods of Babylonian, Sumerian, and eventually Greek. The Greeks were the most powerful, or at least that's how they told the story, and they didn't like the idea of being fodder for a war against a bunch of aliens from another solar system, so Zeus led them in rebellion and seized their power. Naturally, they were jealous. Some of their children and grandchildren settled elsewhere and created other pantheons across the world. Sometimes it ended in blood."

Her story probably qualifies as the strangest pillow talk ever. History's dirtiest secrets laid bare. "OK, where do the Rigellians fit into all this?"

"Ever hear of a little place called Roswell, New Mexico? Just shortly after World War Two?"

The pit in my stomach gets a bit bigger. "Little gray men?"

"More like seven-foot-tall, four-armed, yellow and magenta Rigellians on a scouting mission. Now the Olympians, well, they knew most of the

Titans' little tricks, but they didn't know about the thing they left in orbit, because they were a bunch of fucking ignorant savages who offed some alien scientists and absorbed their psionic energy."

"They had Apollo's Chariot?" This generation of Olympians has used it to go to the moon on several occasions. They make regular supply runs to the three active space stations. I even got to ride on it once on the trip that ended in my faked death.

Ah, the shit I would get into if I had my own spaceship.

"And no real inclination to use it. They hadn't left the island in six hundred years until the satellite in orbit started broadcasting to them and the Rigellians showed up."

"Hermes came and got the bodies and the others tried to figure out the thing in the sky. They didn't have to wait long. The construct entered orbit and disintegrated. It caused the super-powered beings. It was some kind of final solution, to elevate all of humanity for some kind of last stand if the Rigellians showed up to finish their former masters. Of course when the Titans built it, all of humanity consisted of less than a million people, so the effects were diluted."

"But what about the rumors of supers that existed before Roswell? A genetic legacy from the original Olympians and their offspring."

"That's the running theory, but you know as well as I do that there were few and far between. There are still at least a couple of Titan things around, some kind of flying probes that 'upgrade' specimens and unlock their potential. At least one is still active. Keisha is the only one of us quick enough to have seen it. We've been trying to capture it for study, when we're not trying to save the world. It's a side project."

"Yeah, it gets a little distracting at times. How many people know about this?"

"The Rigellians? Some heads of government, a few hush-hush agencies, a handful of heroes besides The Olympians, Gravmatar and whomever he has told, and now you. The drone thing? The Olympians and you, unless someone else on my team has let it slip."

I take a moment to ponder if Larry's extremely powerful brand of telekinesis would be able to snatch that probe out of the sky, no matter how fast it can move.

"Gravmatar?" I ask about the exiled Rigellian prince.

"He is exiled, and we had to fight the Rigellians to prevent them from killing him and laying waste to our planet. They let him live because he's also here to keep an eye on us. There are more Rigellian supers, but the percentage is way lower in their population than in ours. The best theory the people in the know have come up with is that the Four Arms are keeping us secret from the other alien species so they can keep watch us and see if we turn into an asset or a liability."

"Well, that doesn't make me feel terribly safe," I add.

"Welcome to my world," Stacy says after a hollow laugh. "But you wanted to know. I'd love to grow old with you, but that's not going to happen."

"Did Patterson know about you?"

She gives a major sigh. "Really? That's what you are thinking about right now!"

I shrug and run my free hand through her hair. "I'm a small, petty man."

"If he did, it didn't come from me. He and I never became serious enough to have this discussion," she states and looks at me. The guarded half-smile she is wearing opens back up to the real thing. "Take some time to think over the future of our relationship, knowing what I can and cannot give you, Cal. If you still want to put a ring on this finger sometime in the future, I won't say no."

Sensing the tone is too serious, I go for my sarcastic wit. "So in a few thousand years, you'll look back at me like the crush you had in kindergarten?"

"More like that guy I fell for at summer camp in third grade," she says. "I'll tell all the other Olympians that you're from Canada and don't really come around anymore. You know something? Why do Canadian guys and gals always get such a bad rap for being the long-distance relationship fakes? That just doesn't make sense. Who do the Canadians use? Do other countries use Canadians for scapegoats as well? That just doesn't sit well with me."

Stacy goes off on these odd rants every now and again. Obviously, I'm attracted to her wit as well. It's a total turn-on, and I kiss her.

"You still OK with all this, Cal?"

"It's just another obstacle. When all this calms down, I guess I'll need to start looking into ways of extending my rather questionable existence. Maybe I can actually program my brainwave patterns into something like Andy's body, or magic might have an answer. Heck, if all these legends are true about gods and whatnot, maybe the fountain of youth really exists. If one of your buddies decides they have had enough of the whole Olympian lifestyle, I could take over."

"The older Olympians died within a couple of weeks after transferring their powers. I don't see it happening. The only time it happened with us was on our second mission when our first Hephaestus died and his brother received the transferred powers."

"But not even with Holly. She really likes me."

"She liked that you were dead. She is fairly certain the imposter is you."

"Some goddess of wisdom there for you."

"Seriously though, Cal, wisdom? Not really a defining trait for you."

"I guess you're right. So which one would I be a good fit for? Super speed? Master inventor?"

Shaking her blonde mane, she chuckles and says, "Definitely not Hermes. Well, you're a bit of a homebody, so I'm actually leaning toward Hestia over Hephaestus."

"Hearth and home for the win, baby! If you guys can have a female Hermes, you could definitely have a male Hestia."

"You're not completely sane, Cal."

"Finally noticed that, huh? I guess I should let you slide because you're really just some jumped-up super baby. I guess I really am good with kids. Want me to change your diaper or do you need a spanking?"

"Ha. Very funny. Does that make you a cradle robber?" She reaches around to my backside and gives me a stiff swat on the rump. It kind of hurts given how strong she is.

It isn't really that funny, but irony makes for a good defense mechanism and gives me the time I need to process all of these revelations. The idea of the Rigellians out there watching us and trying to decide if we might be useful allies or need to be put down before we become a threat doesn't excite me any more than my girlfriend being a couple of centuries short of super-puberty.

Shit! I remember when the biggest problem I had to deal with was planning a bank job or Patterson's lawyers making my life miserable. When did it become so complicated?

Chapter Five

When a Big Reveal Flops

For all the nasty things I've done in my life, I actually sleep fairly well. In that respect, and pretty much everywhere else, I am probably far luckier than I deserve to be.

This morning I am regretting the topics Stacy and I covered last night. There were some harsh and bitter truths that I have been ignoring, even if on some level I actually knew that my godly girlfriend would still be kickin' it long after my bones had crumbled to dust.

Mortality looms like an ugly cloud around my bed this morning. Of course all the talk about Olympians, Titans, and all those unmentionables' secrets probably aren't helping my not-so sunny disposition.

"Are you OK, honey?" Stacy asks.

I know enough not to try and argue with an impasse. Fat lot of good it will do me.

"I'm just trying to wrap my mind around it. There was a time when the most difficult thing I had to face was trying to plan a bank job. Now, I am a father, and I just got a primer on all the dirty secrets no one should have to know. I guess I should put on my big boy pants today."

She pulls me into a hug and says, "I have been stringing you along for too long. I didn't want to leave anything out there and have any more secrets between the two of us. You'd be surprised how much keeping this from you has been tearing me up inside."

"Does that mean all the guys on your team can't get it up? Or are they just shooting blanks?" Yeah, I went there.

The former is funny and might be useful down the road, but the latter is just kind of sad. I could probably start calling them the Infertiles instead of the Olympians.

"Blanks," Stacy answers. "All of us have done some checking with some of the most world-renowned fertility specialists, but even fancy genetic engineering can't get around our physiology. It hit Robin the hardest because she was engaged and looking forward to building a life with her fiancé after she graduated college, but our little adventure to the hidden island of the Olympians flushed all her dreams down the crapper."

"Damn! Hera is one of the few on your team that I respect. At some point, would you be up for adopting some kids? I know all you really cool celebrity types dig that kind of thing. It might be good for your image unless the public finds out who the adoptive father is. Then you're pretty much screwed."

Touching her chin, she thinks it over for a minute before saying, "I won't rule it out, but just like Wendy found out, any new additions to a family of a superhero become a vulnerability that the villains can come after. Give me some time to really consider it before I give you an answer, if that's OK?"

"Take all the time you need. I just wanted to throw it out there as a possibility. I'm not ready to outfit the Megasuit with a cane or a walker just yet, so I think you've got some time. How about we take the rest of this discussion into the shower and I will be your personal shampooer for the morning."

"I believe that is a deal I can readily accept. Race you to the shower!"

It's just my luck that she is asking at the same time she is already out of bed and on the move—damn cheating wench!

• • •

Stacy's suit is called The Centurion and it is based off my old Mark II armor. I have nothing to do with the stupid Roman motif for an avatar of a Greek goddess. I will seriously bite any fingers that are pointed my way. Her marketing people have to take the blame for that stupid shit.

"I keep thinking I should start calling you Venus since you want to be Roman now."

"Funny, Cal. I lobbied for naming it Spartan, but the handlers thought that sounded too warlike. Centurion makes people think sentry and safety."

Digging around in her suit's innards, I grumble. "Things like that are important in your world. I get it, but really we're mixing pantheons here; that's offensive to anyone who likes history. Hoplite. You could have called it a Hoplite!"

Stacy chuckles. "Whatever! Most people would think it is some kind of bunny suit. You're just being a history snob. Get over it! All I am saying is that the name was focus-group tested and the people like it. You're just gonna have to suck it up, Buttercup!"

I pause and pull my head out of the armor's chest. "You're just waiting for me to make some innuendo out of your last sentence, aren't you? Well, I'm not going to fall for it. I'm a much more mature Cal Stringel."

"Keep telling yourself that," she deadpans. "You're not fooling anyone."

"I've got your Hoplite right here," I say and toss a crude gesture her way.

"You're much more mature Cal lasted all of five seconds. I think that's a new record for you."

"You bring out the kid in me considering you should be running around in semi-immortal pull-ups right now."

She is enjoying our back-and-forth as much as I am. "I will have you know that I'm getting an honorary degree from Embry Riddle next month and I'm going to show up in armor so all those aerospace engineers can drool over it, so let's see something special!"

"I think UCLA rescinded my actual degrees when I went to prison. Maybe the imposter will get them to reinstate what I've earned. I heard they want the fake to appear on campus since he's running his scam out of Hollywood right now."

"Actually, I think they were restored after you died," she replies, making air quotes on the last word. "You must not have gotten the memo, being deceased and whatnot."

"Oh," I continue, somewhat surprised I had missed that infonugget. "Guess I was too busy with my whole dying thing to notice that one. I'm back to being wise and learned Cal again. Well, I hope you enjoy your trip to sunny Florida. Are you going to swing by your old school on the way?"

"Probably."

Stacy attended Rollins College in Winter Park—double major mathematics and elementary education. Had fate, and apparently alien-empowered Greek gods, not interfered, she would have been the crush of preteen boys in some little school out there. Instead, she's the crush of damn near everyone on the planet, a crush who has to shoulder the weight of the world and be a positive role model for all to see.

I know she sometimes wonders if that wouldn't have been a better life. The only thing people would say about my being a positive role model is that they would be positive I shouldn't be one.

"The fake shield generator will go in your forward arc. If you're close to losing your shields, we'll signal you from here. That should give you enough time to pivot out of the way and we can hot swap a spare into your armor for some instant reinforcement."

"Nice. Are you going to touch the weapons systems?"

Oh, a bonus request! "You've got the one force blaster and thorax-mounted sonics for crowd control. Are you looking to get more offensive? I could give you some serious teeth."

"I'm not sure, but I'd like to have more options. Plus, since you have power to spare coming into this suit, it wouldn't hurt to add some more energy-based weapons. I suppose my own railgun is out of the question?"

I can't fault her for dreaming big, but asking for her own railgun? Seriously?

"Unfortunately, the base can't support the requirements right now. Plus, that's my signature weapon . . . no touchy!"

"Possessive much?"

"As a matter of fact, yes." I notice some loose wiring that needs to be secured; sloppy work on my part, but in my defense I built this suit out of what little I had in this base at the time. Then again, it could have gotten loose during regular use, so maybe I'll wait and see how this next week plays out before committing to designing a new weapons suite.

"I went light on the synthmuscle because of your natural strength; do you want me to do it right this time? It might make things a bit more cramped in there than you're used to."

"Will that satisfy your tinkering needs?" Stacy asks.

"Probably not, but it should tide me over for now. We have to discuss a small matter of payment."

"No good girlfriend discounts?"

"Actually, I would be more inclined to hand out a bad girlfriend discount, especially if you're naughty. Seriously though, without access to Wendy's money and with no real legal standing, I need you to do some spare parts shopping if you are up for it?"

"Depends on what you need," she states thoughtfully. "Delivery van-sized order? I can probably swing without any major problems. If you want a full semi worth of stuff, that might be an issue."

The Love Goddess drives a hard bargain, but I take what I can get.

"So how is Paper Tiger fitting in with your team?"

"He's not, really," I reply. "Phipps is kind of boring, if you ask me. His power is cool and he really can get around, but that's about it."

"So you're not looking to have him join your garage band anytime soon?" she asks, referring to one of the ways we pass the time down in the base. I've spent so much time practicing on my drum set that I'm as good as I ever was back in my college days.

"I'm still holding out for you joining. We need the hot chick to expand our demographic, and Wendy can't play and her singing cries out for auto tune. How's your singing voice?"

Stacy does the universal "so-so" gesture with her left hand. "I took piano when I was younger, but hiding the hot chick behind a keyboard defeats the purpose of objectifying me like that."

Considering she's a super powered quasi-immortal, my girlfriend is refreshingly down to earth.

"Yes, that does present a problem."

"I could learn the keytar. It's high time for that to have a comeback."

"I'm having 'My Prerogative' flashbacks now. If you're going that route, why not be the woman playing the saxophone instead?"

Stacy shakes her head and sadly says, "I hate to burst your bubble, but I'm pretty sure she wasn't really playing."

"No! No! Don't you dare kill the fantasy! What the hell were we talking about again before we got sidetracked with this?"

"I was asking about Charles fitting in," she says. "Or something like that."

"Oh, that's right. Long story short, with José gone, he's spending more time with the Gulf Coasters tracking down leads and participating in that ever-popular monitor duty. I really miss that crap!"

"Easy on the sarcasm, honey."

"Most days, it's all I know," I reply and walk over to the workbench. I finish the list in my hands and compare it to the screen of our available inventory. I will have to be tight on my synthmuscle to make it last. "Andy can break all this out of storage. Ready for a surprise?"

"Lay it on me, Cal."

I walk over to where my neural interface suits hang and select the one with my magic belt on it and drop my shorts.

"Not exactly a new surprise," she says, looking over my naked form as I pull on the suit. "Been there, done that."

"Yeah, yeah. You're pretty acerbic for someone who is supposed to be the world's girl next door. You know that, right?"

"Did you run out of fabric to cover your ass, or are you going for the techno-cowboy chaps look? I didn't bring any dollar bills with me, so if you're going to be doing any dancing, you might be disappointed. If we can get Bobby in his motorcycle jacket, Larry in a sailor suit, and Andy as a construction worker, you'd be well on your way to being a Village People cover band."

"You're so mean! However, I am in an unusually good mood today for some reason, so I'm gonna let that slide. Are you ready to be astounded?"

"As ready as I can be."

I chant under my breath and begin the transformation, letting the ancient dinosaur magic slither across my body. My best time so far has been twenty-two seconds. It's not painful anymore, merely uncomfortable.

Finished, I pivot and swish my short tail. "Needed the opening for this," I say with a definite hiss in my voice. "What do you think?"

"OK, you look like a Mangler in techno-cowboy chaps. Pretty cool, but I'm not sure what it gets you."

"Increased reaction time, better balance, and the utter awesomeness of being the only armor-wearing dinosaur/human hybrid mage in existence."

"You really do have a lot of free time on your hands, Cal. Maybe too much," she says.

"You no likey?" I ask, and it sounds utterly ridiculous in my current form. She looks underwhelmed. Maybe she is mad that my winky virtually disappears in this form.

"It's interesting," she replies and pauses, obviously searching for the words to say what she means without pissing me off. "I just don't see the benefit yet."

"Well, if I can figure out how to hide the belt, I can pass for a Manglermal and maybe infiltrate them. It might get us closer to José. With the fake running around out there, who would connect me with Cal Stringel? I might as well get some of mileage out of all this and whatnot."

Stacy nods in agreement. "OK, that makes sense, or at least as much as I can take today. How strong are you like that?"

"I can lift about five hundred pounds, better reflexes, and I suppose I'm a better climber; but I invent jetpacks if I need to do any climbing. All in all, it's not that spectacular, but it's more than I could ever manage on my best day. You still don't like it, do you?"

"Would it make you feel better if you knew I had a fear of lizards and snakes as a kid?"

"A little," I answer. "Is there a funny story connected to it?"

"Not really. More like a six-year-old girl screaming her ass off."

"Bummer."

"Well, you could get some of those parachute pants to hide the belt and be a late-eighties rapper. Just give me a warning before you do, so I can gouge my eyes out."

It's probably as close as I can get to a compliment out of her right now.

"I thought you'd like it." A lizardman hissing a whiny line like that. It's not a sight often seen.

"I like that you are still exploring Tyrannosorcerer Rex's magic, and it would put you on even terms with any Manglermals you came across, but I like the real Cal Stringel, not an imposter, and not dinosaur enhanced. If you're fishing for compliments, then yes, you really have something unusual here. It's really out there! Seriously. What I don't want you to do is stop experimenting and tinkering. Your persistence is what makes you amazing, and not always the results you achieve."

I can't help smiling through her somewhat backhanded compliment. Stacy can lay it on thick when she needs to.

• • •

Andy's new robot body is another project I've been working on, and it isn't going well. I'm not exactly guilt-ridden over this, but if we are being honest, I am struggling with making it. Andy has moved on to practicing subtlety, and by practicing I mean dropping hints about how much he has done around here and how much more he could do if properly equipped.

My normal creations lack elegance but make it up for it in destructive power. I'm just not an artist like Doctor Albright. Anything sturdy enough by my standards looks like so much industrial crap, and the efforts that appear nice with tight lines are just too damn flimsy.

I'm cheating as much as I can with mirror fragments providing power and freeing up room in the design, but it doesn't seem to be coming together at all. Sucking at something dredges up all my old memories of inadequacy.

Maybe I'm overthinking it. I do that a lot.

I've offered to go bust up some of Andy's siblings and collect some spare parts.

Needless to say, that idea was rejected. My workshop is good, but nothing like Doctor Albright's laboratories. He's able to fold the metal over on itself, many times over, and thicken it to allow human-like shapes that no one else on the planet, not even Patterson's corporation, can match.

Magic can't help me with this. I need better tech to make this happen, and we don't have the space, money, or the ability to shop for the things that would allow me to get in the ballpark of what the leading robotics expert in the world is capable of.

Stacy arrives to witness my technological impotence. "Hey, Cal. Oh, I know that look. What's wrong?"

I regard my girlfriend, fresh from a well-deserved nap. "Got any inspiration to spare? I'm fresh out of ideas and I could use your perspective."

Since she read my book, Stacy knows that she is my personal muse. Her offhand comments have led to some of my best ideas—even one that saved the world.

"OK, break the problem down for me and I'll see if I can think of something fresh."

She listens to my whining and my complaints. I let her mull it over while she inspects my less-than-usable efforts to date. It's like Goldilocks and the three mechanical limbs; none of them end up being just right.

"Well, since you don't have the machinery, and magic is useless, what else do you have to work with?"

"Just us chickens," I answer.

"What about Larry?" Stacy says in a curious tone.

"Beg your pardon?"

She grabs a cross section of metal and explains. "He's a world-class telekinetic. He can take a three-inch-thick sheet of steel like this and crumple it like a used Kleenex. Why not see if he can use his abilities to get you super dense material? Something no press or annealing machine is capable of."

I do my best to try and poke holes in her rather promising theory. "Um . . . that can't . . . well, maybe it could . . . no, it might make the metal too brittle."

"What about carbon fiber, then?"

"That could work," I say. "Maybe a composite blend of the two. You know, I can work with that! You . . . you are a genius!"

She laughs. "I know. But you just want me for my body."

No sense in denying the truth. "That's true, but I appreciate your brilliant mind, too."

"Well, you're always looking for ways that you can cheat, but you are focused on you. Don't forget about the things your teammates can do when you're looking for ways to beat the system. Bring them outside the box with you and all that happy horseshit."

She's right. I do get tunnel vision and am a little arrogant, just a tiny, tiny bit. Every solution doesn't have to come from me. "I can get Andy to run the numbers after Larry does some test compressions to get the right ratio of carbon to steel."

It seems like a great weight has been lifted from my shoulders. I couldn't solve this myself. Then again, Doctor Albright has a staff and a team of highly skilled people. I don't hate the man. . . Hell! I respect Albright for trying to make the world a better place and am jealous of his expertise. Even when I beat Patterson and his army of engineers, I still had help. Maybe that's the lesson I need to learn, because General Devious and The Overlord are still out there, and they never fight fair or alone.

So I won't, either. I have something no one else on the planet has, and I'm going to ask him to hook a brother up!

A new branch of possibilities is open to me—achievement unlocked and all that shit. How tightly can Larry wind strands of synthmuscle? Opportunity knocks, and I need to stretch my legs anyway, so I might as well answer the door.

Sometimes the greatest superpower of all is knowing when to ask for help.

• • •

"I give you . . . Alloy-L!" I scream and hold up a length of the blackish composite material, like I'm Moses showing off the Ten Commandments. *Thou shalt be strong!*

"Can you keep it down, Cal? I've got a splitting headache," the Alloy's namesake says while massaging his temples. "I haven't concentrated that hard in a long, long time."

"Sorry Larry," I answer. "I can finally put a body together for Andy that's worth a damn. This is huge, and I have you to thank for it."

The material is stronger than steel and significantly easier to work with than metal. What I have in my hands is going to be Andy's lower left leg. I am half-tempted to launch into a rousing rendition of "Just A Friend" because I finally have what I need.

"Do we shatter a champagne bottle on it or something?" Wendy asks before adding, "I might miss and hit you."

I point the material at her like a magic wand. "You can try, boss lady, but you're not going to ruin this moment. I'd like to thank the Academy for this award, my lovely girlfriend for the inspiration, Andy for being patient, Bobby for showering, and of course Larry for making all this possible."

"The new material meets all the necessary parameters," Andy states, while Bobby flips me off. "How soon do you anticipate having my new body completed?"

"Two weeks, depending on how much Larry can make at a time. After that, we can move on to making a set of plating to replace the exterior of Megasuit."

Stacy laughs. "But you have all those powerful shields. Shouldn't the next batch be for my armor? I did give you the idea to enlist Larry's help after all."

She's a traitor, but I do have to agree with her—even if I don't want to.

"I didn't know your inspiration came with a price tag, but I suppose you do need more protection in that itty bitty suit of yours. We will have to figure out later how to add different colors to the material and see if we can match the Centurion's current scheme."

"You mean Andy's gonna be a black robot now? Shit! Now he's gonna get profiled by the police all the damn time!"

Everyone in the room, with the exception of the android in question, groans at Bobby's attempt at humor.

"Congratulations, Cal," Stacy says and gives me a congratulatory peck on the cheek. "Unfortunately, I have to get going now."

"Sure you won't stay a few more days?" I ask, already knowing what the answer is.

"Unlike you, I've got a job and people expecting me. I'm sure the tabloids are on the edge wondering where I am."

We all traipse upstairs and ride the elevator up to the surface. Stacy holds Gabby during the short trip and my daughter is already getting fussy. She senses that the Olympian is heading out. I put on a brave face—stoic, very stoic—and reclaim my equally unhappy daughter while the love goddess gives us both a hug goodbye. I am beginning to think that part of Wendy's dislike for Stacy is centered on how much Gabby adores the Olympian.

No jealousy issues there whatsoever. On the other hand, I don't really mind when Paper Tiger holds Gabby. I'm not threatened by an animated drawing of a tiger. It's a bonus when Gabby yanks on his whiskers. That shit has to hurt!

The base is going to feel empty soon. Bobby has a lead on one of Larry's baby mammas, so Bobby is once again becoming The Highwayman. Larry is taking a couple of days off right after we finish our first full-production run of Alloy-L. Phipps is headed back to the Gulf Coasters and then to South America again to search for José. Wendy is actually going to Havana, where she plans to meet secretly with her mother in what can be considered "neutral territory." Mrs. LaGuardia is hoping to broker some kind of deal where Wendy can go back to the real world. I'm on the fence about that. Wendy can drive me up the wall and vice versa, but if she is here, so is Gabby.

Both Wendy and I have our doubts, but the boss will have Megasuit there to back her up, and there will be plenty of foreign press there for Wendy to speak to without U.S. interference if this deal never materializes. It's also time to go on a PR offensive against the fake Cal Stringel. That asshole has been running his mouth and stirring up trouble. Either fake Cal has adopted Megan Bostic's anti-superhuman stance or she is using him to advance it. Wendy's pappy is using both of them as well.

The base will feel lonely with just me, Gabby, Andy, and his two robot puppets about, but there're things to be done and anthills that need kicking over.

Trouble isn't likely to come to our little corner of Alabama, so we need to stretch our legs and go looking for it.

I suspect it won't be too hard to find.

Chapter Six

Sometimes a Naked Woman is a Bad Thing

Havana is an interesting city, almost trapped in a time loop, and not a good one, either. It's run down, and a decade's worth of economic embargo has taken its toll. I don't really care about a missile crisis from times gone by. Face it! That might have been one of the first times that the world teetered on the brink of destruction, but there have been a slew of them since.

Maybe it's just the realist in me. If the ruling brothers were more of a threat, they would have been dealt with by now. There's a rumor going around that they might be supers themselves, but it's never been proven.

Either way, it doesn't matter to me. A place is a place as far as I'm concerned. Plus, when do I get to see so many classic cars out on the road?

The word has gotten out pretty fast concerning our presence. Mega is kind of a sight to behold, and Wendy isn't exactly hiding, either. She's chatting amicably with a pair of the local talents, a man who can control sand and a cybernetic clawed woman. I'm more interested in the modified Type-B robot hooked to a cart filled with sand.

Fernando is trying to impress us by making sculptures in his sandbox as we head to the hotel where Wendy is meeting her mother. Unless we are fighting *El Salvadera* on a beach, he's a lightweight, and *La Tejon de Miel* looks more threatening than she actually is. But they're two of the more prominent heroes in this country, and they want to make sure we are properly escorted.

Of course, properly escorted means having a news crew documenting our "historic" visit.

"Our presence is already being reported on the BBC," I say, using my digitized version of Andydroid's voice.

"Won't be long then before DC knows, if they don't already," Wendy replies. "Keep an eye out for Apollo's Chariot. If it takes off, let me know."

"Acknowledged," I state, sticking to the "Andydroid gone wild" story. The Olympians would be the most likely candidates if Uncle Sam tried to send someone after us. They would also be the most likely to refuse that request, because Cuba is a sovereign nation and whatever trumped up charges the government has on us don't warrant an international incident, in Hera's eyes.

I've never really been the source of an international incident— surprisingly enough, I can't cross that off my bucket list, which makes me wonder if your bucket list resets when you are faking your death.

Those are the kind of things that cross my mind when I'm not actively doing something. Trying to be useful, I call up the specs for the hotel where Wendy is meeting her mother and run a few simulations. The results are not terribly helpful.

"It appears you will be on your own, Wendy," I say in a slow and measured tone. "The penthouse will be unable to withstand the weight of the Megasuit. I advise caution and to be wary of the possibility of a shapeshifter."

"We have a set of code phrases, but I will leave my transmitter on so you can hear what's going on. If there's a problem, come running. Either way, stay in the area and be ready to move fast."

I nod. It's either a trap or it isn't. Anyone stupid enough to try it deserves what happens next. Wendy's mom used a cover story that she was down here scouting talent in Cuba for a Canadian production company. To me, it sounds a little convoluted, but hey, I'm just pulling bodyguard duty today.

"Honey Badger," I say using the English version of the woman's name. "I would like to do a scan of your cybernetics sometime before we depart, if you permit. I am always considering upgrades to this suit and lack quality melee options."

The clawed woman, who looks more like a body builder, shrugs at my request. "It's not like bootleg plans of this old Spetsnatz tactical gear aren't all over the Internet. I've fought over a dozen in the past five years. Almost any idiot with half a million U.S. could build one in their garage these days."

"True, but this is one of the original sets produced in the 1980s, and it has stood the test of time quite well, thanks in part to your own body density manipulation abilities." She was correct. I'd even built a knockoff set back in the day, but it would be interesting to analyze one of the originals.

The Cuban superhero has the ability to harden her skin to the point that it is nearly impenetrable, which seems like a handy ability to have if you ask me. She doesn't quite get to the point of Seawall's invulnerability, but by the same token, she isn't a walking douchebag like he is. The other reason I want to take a good hard look at her gear involves Seawall. If the U.S. government can effectively replicate his powers, even for a few minutes, I suspect I'll see them outfitted with things like this.

Unfortunately, the real Andydroid hasn't cracked those little patches that Uncle Sam was developing in conjunction with Seawall. I'm looking forward to trying one out sometime. I could just picture the conversation:

"I didn't know you smoked, Cal."

"Nah, I'm on the invulnerability patch. Possible side effects include vomiting, nausea, and turning into an all-around raging dickhead."

"Something funny?" Fernando asks me.

I'm sorely tempted to start playing a certain ABBA song, but that would be too easy. I need something better.

"Oh, I am trying to emulate human actions," I say, in an effort to cover and not draw the ire of Wendy. "My subroutine indicated that I should choose a random action. In this case, it was a chuckle. I considered belching, but that seemed inappropriate, and I have not decided if I should add an odor component to them."

"Andy, knock it off," Wendy says in a terse fashion, and I realize that my save failed to prevent the wrath of my team leader. I will definitely hear about that one later. She will ask about that vocal cutoff switch again. Somehow, I never get around to making it. Wonders never cease.

As far as Wendy is concerned, I am quite possibly the worst actor ever. Bobby is always trying to convince me that I should have been the leader and never recruited her. On occasions like this, I actually entertain the thought, but leading is too much responsibility. Cal Stringel and any form of the word "responsibility" usually don't go well in a sentence together, unless it's an accusation like "Cal Stringel, are you responsible for this mess?"

"Understood," I say and cut off my external microphone. Sometimes, it is actually best to be seen rather than heard. I'm sure Wendy would agree with that sentiment.

Maybe I could run the burp through the copy of my friend's sonic bugle in the thorax to get something that would shake the nearby windows?

I really do come up with the oddest ideas when I am bored.

"This is where we separate," Wendy says. "Stay out of trouble and don't make me regret bringing you."

It's a throwaway line, she already does. Ha ha! Points for me!

Honey Badger escorts Wendy into the hotel, leaving me in the company of The Sandbox. He seems disappointed that I'm his assignment. I would prefer the woman with the tech over the guy who uses his robot as a sand bucket. Although I do see a drop-down undercarriage turret with twin plasma rifles, so maybe Fernando isn't a complete tool.

Ah, the pitfalls of the hero lifestyle and all that jazz.

Did I mention that I don't really like jazz?

I try to stir up some conversation with The Sandbox centered on whether the sand in his converted robot fouls the internals of the plasma rifles and whether he would be better served by using sonics.

Gawd! I'm turning into the effing Bugler!

Wendy's conversation with her mom makes me almost wish for a shapeshifter. There's a mixture of "I'll support you whatever you do" and "Are you sure you know what you are doing?" Politicians have fewer flip-flops.

Fortunately, Wendy is not some shrinking violet and can go toe-to-toe with the strongest beings on the planet. Even if she doesn't know what she's doing, she will make it work out in the end.

And ultimately, that's why she's in charge and not me.

Fernando actually is interested in my idea about sonics and confesses that the sand does really hamper his weapons, which sort of makes me feel even worse, but there are worse ways to pass a few hours. Fortunately, I'm really back in the base and have all the diversionary wonders of the Internet at my disposal. When the conversation lags and drops off after forty-five minutes or so, I cut off my external microphone and queue up one of my playlists. Instead of the fearsome foursome from Sweden, I go a different route and put on Bad Company just because it fits more with the theme of today. I could never convince my college band to do a cover of it. Instead, it was Bob Seger this and Bob Seger that. Hey, I like the man from Detroit as much as the next guy, but how many people in Southern California were crying out for a Seger cover band at the time? I wouldn't even call it a niche market, it was so small.

For old time's sake, I line up "Still the Same" to follow it, because that is still my favorite one of all his hits.

More time passes, and I've resorted to playing ABBA while Fernando signs autographs and entertains his fans with his power. Based on two-guy/two-girl bands, I'm running a simulation of a steel cage Deathmatch between ABBA and Fleetwood Mac, and I'm rather disappointed at seeing them lose to the Europeans.

"Contact!" Andy warns. "High-speed approaching just above sea level. Five miles out and closing from due north. The target passed a weather detection buoy and alerted me."

"What is it?"

"Too slow to be a missile," Andy says. "Attempting to get a fix."

"Wendy!" I cut over to her channel. "Something's coming. Not big enough to be a plane and too slow to be a missile. My guess is that it is one of our kind. I'm moving to intercept. Better wrap things up quickly and get your mother to safety."

"Mom! We have to get the fuck out of here, now." I hear Wendy shift from calm daughter to her "command" persona. The lady knows how to flip the switch.

"Possible enemy on approach," I announce loudly to my escort. "Switching to combat mode. You will need to clear the streets. I will investigate and intervene before they reach the shore."

"*Sí!* I will get to the beach and back you up there."

"Agreed."

Sandbox starts shouting for everyone to get out of here while I activate my jets. He looks a bit nervous. I can't blame him. After all, how many heroes and villains come down to this island to throw down?

I accelerate and start searching for my quarry. I don't have to look far—a powersuit.

Magnify.

It's the Canadian chick, Amanda-what's-her-face, in her Promethia-provided Protector armor. What the hell is a West Coaster doing here, and what does she want with us?

I don't suspect it is to fight, because she'd have brought her whole team, and I can't see the angle where they'd be willing to start an international incident. Opening a channel, I broadcast a simple greeting to the woman. Her seven seconds of precognition is a bothersome power, but I've beaten her before and I could do it again. Although underestimating someone who can see the future is a recipe for disaster.

"Megasuit! I'm glad I found you! I need to warn you about the Overlord's trap."

"What is this about a trap?" I ask as the woman approaches. I switch to just hovering.

She draws closer. "He knows Wendy is in Cuba. He has people staged there already. They could be attacking at any moment."

I have Andy relay the warning to Wendy and motion for her to follow. "We should get back to the others so you can tell us all at once."

"Lead the way," Amanda replies.

The moment I turn around, my sensors detect a massive energy spike. I divert what power I can to the back arc, but she went full on Alpha Strike on me.

The force blasters hit every bit as hard as when I fought Lazarus Patterson's final Ultraweapon suit, and Mega takes a dive down toward the shore from the force.

But my shields hold. Bad news for The Protector as I level out and turn on my new enemy. Andy updates Wendy while I prepare a suitable counterattack.

The next blasts strike my front shields and barely cause any damage, and I wonder if her seven seconds of precognition lets her know how badly she failed.

"Is this the Overlord's trap? It is rather ineffective."

"Pity." The voice switches from female to male. "I was hoping for more. Hello, Tin Man."

It's not The Protector. The Overlord spent years harassing Patterson by making his armor look like Ultraweapon and committing various crimes from robbery all the way up to murder.

Apparently, the M.O. stays the same. I return fire and hit the Donkey Kong switch on my console to start powering up the railgun, but something's wrong. It's too easy. I start a scan of the nearby area, figuring that I need to find whatever other toys he's brought with him—probably a ballistic missile submarine around here.

Andy cuts over on the private circuit. "It is someone else in the armor. A carrier signal is being bounced off several communications satellites."

OK, maybe his M.O. has changed slightly. The suit dodges my first four shots before the fifth tags it. I keep up the pressure and try to drive the armor to the beach. I'd rather interrogate the pilot and see what I can learn.

Since it's not The Overlord himself, I do a deeper scan to see if I can see what's really going on. The armor flying around is a cheap copy of an expensive copy of the Ultraweapon suit. The weapons are top shelf, but the rest of the suit is more on par with my Mark II Mechani-Cal suit—in other words, not that great.

"You are not in the suit, Mr. Orlin," I say. "Who is your lackey today?" I miss the next two shots on purpose to keep the suit moving the way I want it to. Just call me a sheepdog, because I'm herding my opponent right now.

"I would have thought you would have figured that out more quickly, Tin Man. Perhaps your cybernetic mind has been weakened by playing the part of that oaf Stringel."

Hey! I resemble that oaf, and I'm not playing!

I don't bother answering since I have no idea if his power to detect lies extends to long-distance conversations.

"This message is meant for the person in your imitation battlesuit. You should take this opportunity to surrender. Your chance of surviving this encounter will improve significantly."

"OK! OK!" This voice is back to being female with an English accent. "The Overlord has my kids. If I don't try and fight you, he'll kill them! I have to do this!"

A part of me feels bad for the woman. I guess I shouldn't be surprised. He isn't above using people like this. Her force blasters score a couple of hits while I process this. Ten or fifteen more and I might start to worry.

"Just land on the beach and we will sort this out. You will run out of power before you get through my shielding. The Overlord knows this already."

"He's a madman! He'll kill them anyway!"

I don't think Jerimiah is a madman. He's a little too sane for my liking. That's what makes him so dangerous. He wants this woman to beg me for her kids' lives. Otherwise, he'd have shut her up already.

Cutting off the externals, I look at Andy. "Take over the flight path. Dodge her and get us to the beach. We'll try and disable her armor there. See if you can find any English women who work for the Overlord."

Andy nods, and I sense him take over a portion of Megasuit. A few years ago, giving up control of my armor, even the tiniest bit, to anyone, would be like asking me to cut off a finger. I'm more mellow now, at least with Andy, and have embraced the idea of "tagging out" and back in at will. We're an awesome duo! Just don't remind me that Andy is better at operating the armor.

Turning my attention to the weapon systems, I focus on what I can do to overwhelm the armor. Based on what I can guess about Orlin, there's a mighty big self-destruct mechanism inside. The woman or her kids are probably going to die anyway, but anything I can find from the debris might be useful in tracking The Overlord to his base.

"We can jam his signal so that he cannot hear what we and the woman are discussing," Andy suggests. "According to latest estimates, there are at least seven women with English accents that are potentially employed by The Overlord."

It sounds like a good addition to the half-formed plan I have. "Yeah, let's do that!"

Andy starts a broad-spectrum jamming as we pass over the sand. The imitation armor drops like a rock.

Maybe I'm not the only one dabbling in remote control?

I land next to her and divert energy from propulsion to shielding.

"If you can hear me, I will try to get you out!"

I barely get the words out before the armor detonates. It is a pretty strong blast; the armor suffers a thirty-seven percent shield depletion and one of the shield modules is in danger of failing. That'll cost me a few hours on the workbench reconditioning it.

While I wait for the dust to clear, I note that the extra work The Overlord has caused is bothering me more than the dead English chick. Guess I haven't crossed the "goody two-shoes" demarcation line just yet. Stacy would be mad at me, but I gotta be me.

Much to my surprise, there's a transparent figure at the bottom of the fifteen-foot wide crater. She's also naked as the day she was born.

She doesn't appear surprised. So, she's not a ghost.

Floating up, she glances at Megasuit and looks disappointed. She tries to reach through my shields, but the attempt fails. "I hoped I would have brought down your shields, but I guess that didn't happen."

"Correct. Do you even have children?"

"Of course I do, you bloody hunk of scrap metal. The Overlord has a great daycare program!"

Naturally he does.

"How long can you stay intangible?"

"As long as I want," she says with a slightly distant voice.

"Your clothes obviously did not follow."

"Oh, you're a smart one! Aren'tcha?"

"Got a name on this sarcastic wench?" I ask Andy.

He transfers a picture of a red-haired woman. Her name is Raine Tanner, also known as Hot Streaker. She fits the mold of people with only semi-useful powers that Orlin covets and grooms. Unlike other people with similar powers, she can't take anything into her intangible state, even her clothes. She can spy, but really, Raine is only as useful as a five-foot, two-inch-tall naked woman who can't be touched. One instance where she tried to assassinate Lazarus Patterson comes to mind where she materialized and tried to toss a hair dryer into the large bathtub the bastard was sharing with a pair of models. Pity she didn't succeed. Of course, there are at least two other times when she was caught by security cameras dumping chemicals into milk and orange juice. One of the targets died and the other spent a chunk of time in a hospital room protected by a force field.

In short, she might be buck naked, but she is far from harmless or innocent.

"Ms. Tanner, when you are caught, your children will be taken from you. As I recall, a simple low-level electrical current is all that is needed to prevent you from phasing through a wall."

"They'll never hold onto me," she replies, angry that I would even suggest that.

"Perhaps. Please tell your employer that I am unharmed."

"He figured you'd be," Raine answers. "He said that next time he might use a nuke."

Yeah, I could see that. My shields should stop anything that could be fit into the space inside a suit of armor. "Can you survive a nuclear detonation in your state?"

The woman frowns. "Never tried before, luv. Not exactly sure I'd want to give it a try. Anyway, Jerimiah wanted me to give you a message: General Devious has two facilities where your missing friend might be held. The first is in Central Nicaragua and the other is in Northern Mexico. He made me memorize the coordinates for you."

"Should I ask why he is providing this to me?"

The woman shrugs, not caring about her naked state. "He's never liked Davros and he doesn't approve of her working with both Mangler and the Apostle. Sending you against them will either knock them down a few notches or do the same to you. Either way is fine with him."

When she puts it like that, The Overlord is a pretty twisted bastard. I ask her for the coordinates of the facilities and she gladly hands them over.

"Well, our business is finished. I think I'll be going now. Or are you going to try and stop me?"

"If I do, you will just fade into the ground and flee."

"True," she replies. "Still, it makes a girl feel like she's wanted."

"You are not wanted," I state.

"Aw, I didn't think you had feelings. Try to live with your disappointment."

"Thank your employer for me. Hopefully, once I have beaten the General, she will have the locations of some of The Overlord's facilities. I will be sure to let her know the source of my information."

"Do whatever you wish. I've delivered my message and now it's time for me to go. You be a good little android and take care of things, and when you're doing that, remember that you're doing his bidding. He gets a kick out of irony."

The naked woman laughs at me and begins walking toward the nearby buildings. She'll walk through them to lose me. If necessary, Hot Streaker will even sink into the ground and just kind of swim away. Naturally, the inventor in me starts looking for a way to get around her powers.

It's a bit of a pain dancing to The Overlord's tune, but if it helps rescue the Six-Pack, then I'm good with it.

Unless he warns Devious that we're on our way. I wouldn't put anything past the man.

This makes me nostalgic for the old days, when I didn't have the best toy on the block. Back then, people just fought and beat on me straight up without all the subterfuge. Now, I've got Uncle Sam trying to churn out invulnerable super soldiers, suicidal acolytes of the Apostle, and insubstantial women who walk away from me laughing and naked after attempting to kill me.

It feels like an arms race is running, and I don't always know who I'm up against. I do admire The Overlord for one thing—he figured out how to weaponize a naked woman. That's probably not his crowning achievement, but it's got to count for something.

Unfortunately, that makes me wonder what Jerimiah Orlin does consider his crowning achievement, and how soon before I will end up facing whatever that is.

Chapter Seven

Fight Night in Vegas

"I don't like it," I summarize for our leader. "As soon as we get within a hundred miles of either of those sites, he'll tip off General Devious. He's a dick. I'm pretty sure the reason he and Patterson hated each other is that they were too much alike."

Bobby's not back yet. Because of all his commitments to the Gulf Coasters, Charles is really just down to being an occasional guest whom we've let in on some of our secrets. I suspect he and Wendy aren't doing so well, but it's not really my place to ask her. It would also mean that I give a shit, and since we were never really an item, I don't.

"He is forcing us into a crucible," Andy offers.

I definitely would never be caught uttering that sentence, but at least he is agreeing with me.

Wendy gives me the stink eye. "Of course it's a trap, and he's probably got an operation ready to go as soon as he's sure that we are committed."

"Maybe we shouldn't act on the information and screw with him?" I ask. In my life, I've never had many "gift horses" to look in the mouth. I usually end up with gifts from the other end. "Who knows if both those places are being used by Devious and Apostle?"

"I don't want to pass up a chance to rescue José," Wendy replies. "Andy is doing his best to get satellite images of the two places. How's that coming anyway?"

She must be concerned, I think. *She hasn't cussed once during this entire conversation.*

Our android teammate provides the answer. "There is considerable foot and vehicle traffic at the Central American location. I was able to identify three Manglermals at that site. The one in Northern Mexico has averaged only ten percent of that traffic."

"Sounds like Nicaragua then," I say. "We could give the other location to Stacy and have them hit it at the same time."

"Not bad, Cal," Wendy says. "I'm still worried about whatever The Overlord is going to try. Why don't we have Stacy tip off the West Coast Guardians and keep the Olympians in reserve to respond to whatever The Overlord is planning?"

"Any specific reason you want the West Coasters on the frontline instead of the Olympians? I'm the first to admit that with one notable exception, I'm not the Olympians' biggest fan, but I trust them a whole lot more than I do Patterson's bootlickers to get the job done."

Wendy casually answers, "We suspect it's going to be a trap. Why not send the jackasses who tried to arrest me and turn me over to the feds?"

I have to give her credit for that one. Maybe I'm a bad influence on her. Part of me wants to make sure that one of Gabby's parents is a respectable human being, but I'm actually rather impressed with my baby's mama right now.

Larry shrugs and sips his coffee. "I'm not the biggest fan of those assholes either, but make sure Stacy tells them up front they might be headed into an ambush."

OK, maybe Gabby can settle for having a pretty cool uncle to offset her terrible parents. Wendy never got around to naming godparents. Of course, if Larry ever locates any of his kids, he may not have time for my daughter. Andy is probably the safest, if somewhat unconventional, option.

Would that make him a goddroid?

"Daydreaming there, Cal?"

Busted!

"Huh?" Eloquent comeback. I'm on fire!

"Nice to see this is keeping your attention," Wendy mutters. "I was asking you to let Aphrodite know when you go downstairs and connect up to your damn suit."

"Oh! Sorry." I don't bother with saying it won't happen again. It will. I can't help it if the thoughts in my head are more interesting than the crap they're going on about. "Yeah, I'll let her know. Andy? Can you signal her and see if she's in her suit?"

Andy nods and does as I request. My guess is she isn't in her suit right now. She said something about visiting her parents either today or tomorrow. Stacy wouldn't need to bring her suit with her unless she was going to reintroduce me to her parents as her boyfriend.

It would be fun to watch the fireworks . . . almost.

After a couple of minutes with no response from Stacy, Wendy declares our morning meeting over and goes back to her room to see if Gabby is awake. Larry heads for the elevator and says that he is going to stretch his legs.

All that's left are me, Andy, and my thoughts on my girlfriend.

Secretly, I feel bad for Stacy. She loves her parents dearly and has the kind of relationship with them that I could only dream of with mine. But after she let me in on her nigh immortality, I can see why she doesn't mind spending time with her family. Centuries from now, she'll appreciate it.

I get up and go into the kitchen as my hunger starts to get to me. One of the side effects from using my transformation belt and becoming the world's mightiest dinosaur/human hybrid is that I seem hungrier these days, and I now prefer my steak with more pink in the center than I used to.

Grabbing a box of those thin-sliced frozen steaks, I opt for a Philly cheesesteak. Everyone who says food doesn't solve problems has never had a cheesesteak when they were feeling melancholy.

Life's just better with one in hand.

• • •

"Where is your suit at, Cal?" Stacy sounds like she's in a hurry.

"Well hello to you too, my dear. Did you get my message?"

"How fast can you get to Vegas? Can you meet The Chariot along the way?"

There are thought-provoking questions, and then there are *thought-provoking* questions. "Did you make up your mind about getting married? Getting hitched in our suits is a cool idea. I never realized that you'd be in that much of a hurry that you'd commandeer Apollo's Chariot."

"Be serious, Cal! There's a group of villains attacking Vegas. Or you could try turning on the damn news."

"OK, I suppose I can be serious, but only for you. Which criminal mastermind are we looking at today?"

"It could be General Devious's people, or it could be a large group of villains who thought Tulsa was such a good idea that they decided to take it to the next level and go after Vegas."

"Mini-HORDES or Devious doing something specific? I'm near Austin, Texas. I'll fly near something important so you can get reports of my whereabouts. We wouldn't want this to look too scripted. You want Larry and Wendy there?"

"Larry, yes. Let's keep Wendy on reserve. Her little trip to Havana and all those interviews didn't make her popular with the U.S. government."

"Well, the truth does hurt. Especially when it's their hand caught in the cookie jar," I say.

"Not going to argue that point with you," my girlfriend replies. "Get seen and then make a beeline for Las Vegas. I will let you know when we're getting close and you can have Larry get out, so he doesn't have to fly for too long."

"I'll let him know. I'm sure he'll appreciate the consideration."

"We're leaving in two minutes. Hang on a sec, gotta speak to Athena."

Andy pops up on a split screen while I wait for Stacy to return. "James is on his way to the pond where Larry is fishing, to brief him on the situation. Wendy is watching the news reports I am feeding to her room."

"Let her know that Larry and I will be meeting the Olympians and catching a ride to the action with them. Start making a list of who is there so we know what to expect."

"Understood."

"See if you can find out if the Sin City Sentinels are still in the fight too, and if the West Coast Guardians have scrambled."

"Checking now."

Sometimes I get the impression that Andy is probably already doing all these things, but holds off on giving out the information just to make us feel like we are important to the process. If he ever did become some kind of mechanical equivalent to The Evil Overlord, we'd probably be in serious trouble.

As Mega takes a northwest track over Austin and sets a course for the city that once banned Calvin Matthew Stringel, I keep myself busy getting ready for impending combat. I start by checking the autoloaders, getting the extra shield modules staged, and running diagnostics on the four plasma cannons. I pay special attention to the one that overheated and failed at that camp in Mexico, and I wrestle with the notion of pulling it now and just sticking either a machine gun there, or a forty-millimeter grenade launcher. I could easily make the forecast for parts of Vegas hot and sunny with a chance of a large tear gas cloud wafting down the strip.

Yeah, Stacy would probably appreciate that I'm showing restraint. Plus, I can always switch to High Explosive Armor Piercing if things get shitty.

Looking at the stairs, I don't see Andy or Larry yet, so it looks like some manual labor is in order, except I use the belt to transform into my hybrid form. The equipment I swap in and out of the mirror shards in Mega hangs in harnesses attached to a tracked system overhead. My clawed fingers spin a toggle switch that causes the weapon in question to begin rolling back to the stowed position. My biggest concern is making certain that the power cables don't catch on one of the other weapons . . . like that hasn't happened once or twice before, much to my chagrin.

I amble over to the ready ammo locker, deactivate the internal shield that I hope will save my sorry ass if things go boom inside of it, and withdraw a crate containing thirty-six tear gas grenades. It's considerably easier to carry like this. I mean, I'm a manly guy and all that, but I have mentioned that I'm the kind of guy that will do hours of inventing to ensure that I don't have to do minutes of work.

It's how I roll.

• • •

Eleven minutes into my flight, and with the entire team in the lower level, Stacy notifies me that they're two minute from my position. Larry lets out an audible sigh and slides through the poop shoot. Seconds later, I detect the high-speed approach of Apollo's Chariot. The ancient, alien psionic craft, keyed to the brainwaves of the Sun God's avatar, streaks through the sky toward us and I slow, mostly to make Larry Hitt happy.

"The others aren't necessarily happy that Robin wants to bring you two along," Stacy says over our private channel. "Try not to use the railgun inside the city limits. I don't think that famous neon cowboy sign would stand up to that kind of punishment."

"But he looks so arrogant, like he's mocking me," I complain in a fake whine. "He has it coming! Besides, don't you remember that they replaced it like two decades ago when that Merciless Manitou guy possessed it and used it to fight the Haunted Tank and Thunderclaws? That tore up part of the old strip."

"Oh, you're right. I'd forgotten about that," she confesses. It must be an occupational hazard. I nod to Andy to handle the real conversation while I stick to the private channel, more interested in what my girlfriend has to say than the bartering going on with the rest of Stacy's team.

"What the hell is up with the West Coasters, or should I call them the No-Show Coasters?"

"They refused to discuss what they're up to," Stacy says. "Whatever they're doing, it's supposedly more important than dozens of villains running amok in an area they should be protecting. Suffice to say, everyone is pissed."

Wendy's idea of using them as fodder against Devious is looking dubious instead. I don't really like them anyway, so screw them.

"They assume Wendy is riding inside of the suit," Stacy continues. "I told them the shielding is too thick for me to figure out one way or the other."

"With any luck, the boss lady will be sitting this one out and inflicting her gaze of contempt upon yours truly."

One quick look over at Wendy confirms that she has started already.

"Funny, Cal. You're lisping. I assume you're in your 'Little Winky' form."

"Could you please not call it that?"

"With all the things that come out of your mouth that I let you get away with, you will allow me this," she says in a haughty tone.

I think I've just been put in my place. "You're hot when you're being a bossy wench."

She laughs. "I'm always hot. It's my thing, remember? You'd think with less blood down there, you'd have more for the brain cells and have some better comebacks. Oh, look at the time! I have to go."

She cuts our private channel, leaving me hanging.

Now she's just being mean.

But she's still hot.

The energy dome surrounding Apollo's Chariot retracts and allows Larry and Mega inside. I stand near the edge while Hermes practically drags Larry over to one side. I hope that she is telling him about her search for his children, but I fear she is asking him how to get in touch with the "mysterious" Highwayman. The poor woman is headed for a major disappointment of epic proportions.

Apollo's Chariot is a sight to behold. In interviews, the Sun God has stated that it has some kind of sentience that reminds him of a dog or a horse. Naturally, I wonder if I could imbue something similar to that inside of my armor.

Nah, better to stick with Andy running the suit when I'm not. Now, if I ever rebuild Roller and Floater, I could maybe go down that route. As soon as I put the finishing touches on Andy's new body, I can probably set up Floater Mark II in short order. If I fold the wings, I can deploy it from here out the poop shoot. That'll be a few days of rework, but I can make it happen. Can't let the Bugler show me up with my own designs.

It's a pride thing. Plus, if we increase our use of drones, it might cut down on the desire everyone has to expand our roster and let my secret further out of my control.

Additionally, the day someone shows up with Holly Crenshaw at this base is the day I turn a mindwiper on everyone and I'll start over!

Speak of the devil and she shall appear.

Athena approaches. "Tell me, what do you make of the Los Angeles version of Cal Stringel?"

Andy looks at me and I take over the voice channel. "He is most likely an imposter. His version of events relies too much on a device he refuses to discuss."

"You supposedly think like the real Stringel, which is a step down for you, but why do you say that?"

"If there was a device that could generate sufficient protection from a nuclear explosion at point-blank range, the real Calvin Stringel would already be making a set of armor using that as the basis for his shielding or figuring out how to sell it. Instead, he is earning money on the talk show circuit. It does not follow his past behavior."

"That makes sense, but he did pass a DNA test."

"The most probable explanations are either a shapeshifter or magic. Either would be able to fool your test."

"You're right. Odds are that Stringel left his worthless DNA all over the place and he refuses to be scanned by a telepath. Do you plan to confront him?"

I do my best to let her comment slide. Andy sends me a message requesting to take over the conversation, but I'm not walking away from this.

"Perhaps at some point, but there are more important things than worrying about his true identity—in this case, Las Vegas. As long as he is on the television, I know where he is. The truth will eventually surface."

"He has been more obnoxious than usual. I wonder if he is sleeping with Bostic just because Lazarus did."

Bitch, I think. But as much as I don't want to admit it, my imposter is firmly aligned with Wendy's father's "regulate the Superhuman population" group.

"I do have to ask," Crenshaw states. "Why model yourself after Stringel? The man was a loser in every aspect of life."

Wendy's hand touches my shoulder. I look up at her and she mouths, "Stay calm" to me.

Pausing, I gather my thoughts. "He was successful when it counted. Maybe his lessons in failure taught him how to win when it mattered the most."

She sneers. "He was lucky. Nothing more! You might be powerful in that suit, but you'll never get past all of his shortcomings unless you get rid of the dead weight holding you back."

I'm trying hard to not let her under my skin. Before I can reply, Andy cuts my channel off and takes over.

"Fortunately, the results support my theories and not yours. If you are trying to goad me into some form of action or confrontation, then I would remind you of the human adage about poking the bear. It would be unwise for you to continue this or any other conversation with me."

"Athena! Save it for the actual bad guys." Stacy uses her "outdoor" voice, amplified by her Centurion suit.

The Goddess of Wisdom, and I do mean that in an ironic way, wanders off. Meanwhile, I glare at Wendy, who obviously gave the order. "I can fight my own battles."

"You were getting upset and that risks your fucking cover story! You know I'm right. Let Andy stay on the voice channel until you get off the Chariot."

The part that annoys me the most is I know she's right. "I'm not happy about it," I state for the record.

"And I don't really care. Give it a rest! Despite my gut instincts, I'm sitting this out even though I know I can help, so suck it the hell up, Little Winky."

Yeah, that nickname isn't going anywhere. Thanks a bunch, Stacy!

• • •

Despite being banned for life from Las Vegas, I seem to find myself heading there again. Although I heard they rescinded that after I "died." However like most things related to that, I can't really appreciate my return. To be perfectly honest, I'm not a huge fan of large crowds, and going from hotel to hotel like they're miniature amusement parks only gets me so far.

Instead of taking in a show, or even getting a lap dance, I'm providing fire support while Aries and Hestia are trying to tag team Infernex, Velocizapper, five Manglermals, and Twin Taser Tanya.

High-speed energy balls impact my shielding. VZ and Triple T aren't going to get through in this or any decade, but they're trying to keep me occupied. Infernex is the real threat and has drawn all of the strongest Olympians' attention while Tia tosses a pair of wolfmen aside and wipes camel spit away from her face, courtesy of the Humpback of Santa Fe. The goddess of home and hearth is the weakest, physically, of the twelve, but she makes up for it with her intense training. She knows four different styles of martial arts and knows how to vary them based off her opponent.

"Andy?" I ask. "Have you located Blackjack and Slot Machine yet?"

"Negative," he answers. "They have been missing for over twenty minutes."

"Have to count on them taking care of their own business, I guess." The Sin City Sentinels might have been overrun by this mini-HORDES reunion. I didn't really like the first time I experienced a huge matchup of villains against a bunch of heroes, and I can't say that I'm enjoying this stroll down memory lane that much, either.

There's a lot of shitty bad guys out and about. I should be impressed how General Devious pulled this one together. It makes me wonder what she's really after.

Triple T is a former swimsuit model who got a little chunky after having a kid. After a few-fat shaming incidents and at least one psychotic break from reality, she gave in to her anger in a spectacular fashion, with an exoframe and a pair of tasers. Tanya is still pretty hot, but now wherever she goes men flee instead of staring at her open-mouthed. Let's just say that after she stuns her victims, Tanya drags them off somewhere else to play with them.

And people say I have issues! I don't get it either.

Velocizapper continues to splatter my shields with his high-speed bolts of energy. It's pretty damn annoying. Most any motorcycle off the showroom floor could leave this jackass in the dust, but he gets the bonus of the little water balloon-like gobs of electricity, which are sort of dangerous. It's kind of a jack-of-all-trades and master-of-none situation; he wasn't fast enough to rate on the speed scale or the energy projection scale.

In other words, strictly C-List material supporting an A-Lister like Infernix.

"Are you sure I can't just kill these losers?" I ask my boss.

"Wouldn't send the right message," she answers. "Try to play nice."

"Zapper and Tanya qualify as serial killers," I offer, hoping she'll let me take off the kid gloves.

"But if you show you can do the hero thing without resorting to gore, your little sweetheart will be all impressed."

Wendy's mocking me. She does that an awful lot.

While lending what little help I can to Aries, I advance on the others to help Hestia. If I can't turn these scumbags into blood smears on the side of the Luxor hotel, then I can pummel them into submission.

It really makes no difference to me.

VZ recognizes my change in tactics, and starts pulling his little group out of the way of my charge.

Wendy taps me on the shoulder. "Pull one of your plasma cannons back for a sec. I think I can handle that fucking turdburglar for you!"

She walks up to the mirror fragment where the cannon has backed away and puts the tips of her gloved fingers just through the event horizon.

My wind speed meter surges and VZ along with the Humpback are blown aside.

"It was pissing me off, too," Wendy says. "It probably goes against your religion or something, but break his little speed suit."

I'm not as offended as she thinks. Back in the day, I tried to buy the plans for VZ's speed suit to see if the tech was compatible with my Mark II suit, but the little shit wanted too much. Besides, I prefer strength and protection to synthmuscle sprinting amplified by little rocket pods paired with a glorified bug zapper.

Reaching down, I yank the main power leads on his feeble tech, rendering him as fast as a dickhead wearing thirty pounds of metal. Turning to the remaining villains, I see Hestia has had enough of Tanya, leaving me with the Manglers. I turn on the externals. "Robert Barker was famous for hosting the game show *The Price is Right*. He would usually end each show by reminding the viewers to spay or neuter their pets. I suggest you surrender, now."

They didn't, but they ran off in several different directions. I can honestly say that I've never seen a half-man, half-camel run that quickly.

"Interesting sense of humor you have there," Hestia says, coming up alongside of me. A glance over at Triple T shows that the Olympian has removed the swimsuit model from the fray.

"A side effect of using Cal Stringel as a template," I say. "I suppose you do not approve?"

"He was OK by me," she says, much to my surprise. "I didn't mind him so much. Actually thought he was occasionally funny. Not sure about him now that he's supposedly back. Stacy doesn't think it's him. Now that the riffraff is out of the way, how about you and I flank Infernex and help Frankie put that bastard out of commission?"

"Agreed," I say and glance at Wendy, who is equally stunned. Now I have to move the Olympian into the "Not Necessarily an Asshat" column.

Boss lady gives me the slashing throat gesture and I cut off the external. "Let Andy handle this. I've got an idea."

"What's up?" I ask, trying not to sound miffed that Andy is tagging in to fight the boss at the end of the level after I spent the last few minutes clearing it.

"We all agree that you can pass for a Mangler, right? Get some different clothes on and a tracking device. You're going to help one of those two losers escape and lead us right back to one of Devious's lairs. If we're lucky, you can figure out if José is there and we can send a massive rescue party."

I am conflicted. She wants to send me out there without my suit on, in the middle of a city-wide fight. I'd be practically naked. On the other hand, there's a chance we can find my *hombre* from Mexico.

Why in the hell did I ever ask her to lead this team?

Chapter Eight

Getting a Bad Raptor

"I built the most badass blend of tech and magic so I wouldn't ever have to put my ass on the line again. Now look at me!"

My scales are a blend of light green with pink splotches where I still have flesh. In other words, I look like a six-year-old decided to color a dinosaur with only two colors of crayon.

A baggy pair of cutoff blue sweatpants works for my stubby, partially-formed tail. An extra-long black T-shirt covers the magical belt that gives me the power to hold the transformation. I hadn't really spent much time devising weapons or anything else that my dino/human hybrid form can use, so I rip the trigger guard off a plasma pistol and strap a tazer club to my left thigh. I put on a shield vest just to feel like I have some form of protection. It would be really nice to take those invulnerability patches, but Andy still hasn't cracked the chemical code. We may have to find an actual organic chemist that we can trust.

The most important items I grab are a pair of bootleg mindshields. If there's even a chance I'll cross paths with General Devious, I'll need them.

It will have to do. Wendy gave me a whopping five minutes to get myself outfitted for fieldwork. It would have been nice if she'd mentioned the possibility two weeks ago. I might have had time to whip up something more useful.

"Are you finished yet?" Wendy demands over the intercom. "Infernex is out of commission and Aries wants to head to the next trouble spot."

"Coming, Mother!" I lisp, flicking my slightly forked tongue.

"I got your mother right here! Now move your damn ass!"

Charles must be a patient man ... or whipped. That works, too. For the record, I was under mind control the one time Wendy and I slept together.

Tossing one last furtive gaze around my room for anything that I can use, I decide to go before I start regretting it.

Oh, wait! Too late!

Getting down to the basement, I see Andy has the suit backed between two overturned shuttle vans, supposedly looking for anyone who is injured.

"He'll drop you here," Wendy said. "Wait until Andy is clear and then go rescue a loser. Let me guess, you're going after the swimsuit model?"

"No way. I'm going to use this as an opportunity to paw, or claw, I guess, all over Velocizapper's tech."

"Oh. Forgot about the shiny toy angle."

"Update Stacy, in case I get caught."

"Already done. She wished her 'Little Winky' good luck. Seriously, Cal, be careful out there."

I give her a wave of my claw and I slide down the poop chute into the dry heat of Nevada.

"No further enemies detected in this area. Meet me over there and I will fly us to the next location. Bring Infernex with us and we'll leave the others to local law enforcement," Andy shouts to the Olympians and gives me the thumbs-up gesture with the Megasuit.

He moves away while I continue to crouch.

A minute later, they're airborne, and I can slip out of my hiding spot. I scamper across the street to where Velocizapper had his hands and legs zipped tied around a mailbox, courtesy of Hestia.

"They sent me to get you. You want to get out of here?"

"You bet your scaly ass I do! Cut me loose."

"Yeah, yeah, keep your pants on, Granny!" It takes a couple of seconds for my claw to saw through the plastic bands. "Is your suit still able to function?"

"Shit! I don't know. They messed it up pretty badly. Wasn't expecting to run into those fuckers!"

VZ is a short, thin black guy who is Hermes's second or third cousin. His real name is Omar, and he pretty much sticks to the West coast, so I never really crossed paths with him. He was actually on that cruise where the real Olympians snatched their replacements, but he'd gotten off to do some sightseeing two days before the ship disappeared.

Sucks to be him.

He feels justifiably cheated, like he should've been the new Hermes or something. It probably doesn't excuse the homicides and whatnot, but I can't exactly point fingers at anyone, now can I?'

Then again, I'd be pointing a claw right now. "What about me?" Tanya demands.

"I thought you don't want help from any men."

That even got a laugh out of Velocizapper. I tell him to check his suit out while I go and free the angry model.

"Suit's trashed!" Omar declares as I watch Tanya climb of the wreckage of her crude exoframe. It makes me glad that I'm with Stacy and now have something resembling standards that make insane people less attractive. Back in the day, I'd probably be drooling all over her.

"Is it worth salvaging?"

"Yeah, I can fix it. Gonna take some time though, and money."

"OK, I'll carry it. You lead the way."

"Hey! What about mine?"

Her suit isn't worth my time. "That's a piece of crap. Why should I bother? You can just hop out and blend in with the fleeing tourists."

She hurls a few expletives at me before running off, like I care. Instead, I turn back to Omar. He has a control suit on that would be a bit more difficult to hide in a crowd.

"Which way do you want to go?"

"The Stratosphere," VZ answers. "We'll catch the cargo helicopter they've got hidden on top of the parking garage near it."

"Cloaking field?" I ask. "Won't be worth a shit when it takes off."

Omar gives me an appraising look. "You know your way around tech. Nice. Nah, they got some Boker covering all of them with an illusions. By the time it lifts off, there'll be so much air traffic in the area that no one will be the wiser. Pretty easy when you got all the right codes and emergency air traffic protocols."

It isn't a bad plan. The General has several hidden assets all over the city. More importantly, I'm still trying to figure out what her plan is with attacking Las Vegas. Both she and The Overlord usually have a hidden agenda in their plans.

Testing the Olympians' response time?

Drawing out my team?

The always popular stealing something?

I can't waste any more time on speculation.

With no answers forthcoming, I follow VZ down the strip, the sounds of sirens and explosions surrounding us, seemingly coming from every direction.

I look back over my shoulder to see if Tanya or anyone else is following us as VZ turns to go down a side street. Seconds later, I bump into his back and almost knock him over.

"Hey, watch it!"

Only then do I see what's caused good old Omar to stop in his tracks.

At the other end of the street is Holly Crenshaw, Athena herself. Of all the stupid people to run into in Las Vegas, I find her!

It looks like she's taken a break from the fighting to work her communicator. She looks up and I see her leer at us and smile.

Two big jumps from the goddess of wisdom brings her right by us. "Omar! Fancy meeting you here! I daresay that Keisha will be happy to see you! And you brought a little playmate!"

Dodging her first energy spear, I chuck VZ's suit at her to buy me some time. Her second explodes and knocks forty percent off my shield vest. I go spinning into the wall as Omar is thrown bodily into the side of a minivan. He makes a dent in it and crumples to the ground, unmoving.

Think fast, Stringel!

"I hope you didn't kill him. I need his ass alive!" I scamper over to Omar and check him. Putting the underside of a claw to his throat, I feel a pulse and see he is still breathing. Just to be sure, I stun him with my taser anyway.

When I stand, I see Athena looking at me, energy spear in hand, a curious expression on her face. "No honor among thieves, huh?"

"Give it a rest, Crenshaw," I say. "I'm on your side."

She seems unconvinced. "Tell me another lie, Mangler!"

Time to wind up another rendition of my second favorite song—*the big lie.* I need a name. How about the drummer that my band replaced me with when I left college?

One . . . two . . . three! "I'm Agent Matt Harrell, Homeland Security. My mission is to let this idiot bring me to their base and try to get the location back to my superiors."

"Like I'd believe that."

"Get on your communicator and call S—Aphrodite. I've worked with her in the past. Tell her . . . tell her you're with Little Winky. She knows who I am and will vouch for me."

I want to gouge my eyes out at having to say that.

It takes her a long minute to get confirmation. "Little Winky, huh? She vouches for you. How are you going to handle this?"

"Wait five minutes and call in that you disabled the two of us, but you had to leave us. Devious has helicopters hidden by magic for the getaway. Don't look for the one on the Stratosphere's parking garage, that's where I'm taking jackass here. You might check the roofs of the garages by the other hotels, though. Give me fifteen minutes before you move on those."

Athena sizes me up and seems impressed. "OK, Agent Harrell. You've got your fifteen minutes. Good luck with your mission. You're going to need it. Pretty ballsy, sneaking into a telepath's base."

First I had to use Stacy's pet name for my lizard form, and now Holly Crenshaw is complimenting me. It's been one of those days, and it's not even close to being over.

This is precisely why I don't like going into the field.

She offers me her best guess of how to get from here to the extraction point without running into further trouble while I collect Dumbass and his suit. It doesn't look like Omar will be joining me anytime soon, so I'll have to carry his body and the suit as well.

Just because I can carry several hundred pounds doesn't mean I like the weight on my shoulders.

I suppose there is no use in complaining.

Though it won't stop me from doing it.

• • •

Two of General Devious's armed thugs wave me over to what looks like a pair of delivery vans parked side by side. As I pass around the back, I feel the tingle of magic across my body and I see the loading ramp of a cargo helicopter in front of me.

Ascending the ramp, I shout, "Is there a medic? Omar's injured!"

While I set the damaged speed suit on a bench, a woman with short purple-and-blue-tinted blonde hair, in black BDUs, gestures to a body board. "Set him down here, gently. What happened?"

"Athena knocked him into a van, pretty hard. He hasn't been awake since. I had to leave him for a couple of minutes so I could ditch her and circle back."

I start playing the part of the concerned friend while the medic opens the seal of his control suit and splits it down the middle. She runs her hands down his chest and looks at the bruises on his ribcage. "Possible head trauma. Can't tell if the ribs are broken until we get back to base, but it looks like they are. Pulse is steady, but weak. Get the kit off the wall over there and bring it to me!"

I grab the box and kneel next to the medic. "Is he gonna be OK?"

"Does he have any powers?"

"No, just tech." At least I'm pretty sure he doesn't have any real powers. If I had my armor, I could check the database. Then again, if I had my armor, I wouldn't be having this conversation.

"Tough to say," she answers. "I'll stabilize him for now and we'll take him to the infirmary when we get back, but I'm not going to make any promises. You might be better off just taking him to a hospital. Help me with the straps, we'll secure him to the board for transport. I can stay and monitor him unless we have someone in worse shape."

"Just do what you can," I say and lean down to the injured villain. "You hang in there, buddy. They'll get you fixed up! Just hold tight!"

. . . and the Oscar for best actor in a real-life drama goes to . . .

I recognize a few of the others already sitting in their rumble seats. A very familiar one-eyed woman is looking back at me.

"Who're you? I don't remember you, but you look familiar. We ever work together?"

"Bad Raptor," I answer with a pun on bad wrap. "Or Matt if we're being friendly. I'd remember working with you, She-Clops."

"I didn't know VZ had any Mangler friends."

"He probably doesn't consider me a friend, but I consider him one. He calls me when he needs extra muscle."

"Oh," she says with a look of utter disgust on her face and shakes her left hand from side to side. "Ah, spare me the afterschool special drama. Did you manage to grab anything valuable?"

"Too busy getting him and making it back here."

"Pity," she says and pats the duffle bag next to her. "I was hoping to do some bartering on the flight back to wherever we're headed. I happened to pass by several jewelry stores."

I'm not banking on Jeannie's route being a coincidence. I don't really care, but I remember the not-so distant past where I was a criminal. Criminals almost always are interested in someone else's haul. It's an industry rife with jealousy.

"Got anything good?"

She gives me a distasteful look. "Considering you've got nothing to barter with, I don't think so. Why don't you go crawl into some hole, you filthy animal, before I look at you the wrong way?"

As the other villains around her snicker, I suddenly grasp the reason why so many Manglermals have a chip on their shoulders about being treated like third-class citizens. I'll remember this next time Bobby starts in on She-Clops having a thing for me. She might have held her tongue if I wasn't the only one onboard, but knowing Jeannie like I do, I doubt it.

Still, She-Clops isn't stupid. If she did anything, it might blow a hole in our getaway ride, so it's just an idle threat. I sneer at her and flip my shield vest off and sit across from her next to where the medic is still tending to Omar. Pulling the busted Velocizapper suit in front of me, I ignore the others and take stock of it. The synthmuscle in it is high quality. It has to be to take the pounding. It looks like the bundles are encased in a sheath with a heating mechanism in it to keep the fake muscles at their most flexible temperature.

It's a smart move and prolongs the service life of the synth. Even so, it makes for a hot suit, which is the reason he lobs those little balls of plasma—to get rid of the excess heat.

The suit makes much more sense now, and I appreciate the simplicity of the design. I bet I can build a knockoff pretty easily that Andy could use. Considering how fast he thinks, giving him a speed upgrade would make him infinitely more effective. Hell, give him a tiny mirror fragment for a powerline and a data cable and he could run this suit remotely just like I do.

Seven other villains run up the ramp, followed by the two guards. Both of the guards rush to the cockpit to speak with the pilots. One of the new arrivals is an Ox-Man with his coat dyed blue, carrying what might very well be the large gold nugget from the casino of the same name. I've heard of this guy. He calls himself Babe, as in Paul Bunyan's ox.

The blue ox gives me a nod and says, "Strap in, if you can, or hold on like I'm gonna! Word just came down that they found one of the getaway choppers near the old strip. We're outta here."

The ramp begins to rise and the engines start. Another thing I notice is that the viewports have polarized and darkened, making it impossible to tell which direction we are heading.

At this juncture, I begin to wish I'd grabbed a jetpack. If this chopper gets shot down, I might regret telling Athena about the helicopters, in addition to the whole possibly dying part.

Before I can strap in, the medic asks me to tie the body board with VZ on it down to the eyebolts in the floor. It gives me something to do other than worry about perishing in a ball of flames, so I give her a hand. I even slide the broken speed suit into the seat and strap it in as we take off. It wouldn't do to have that thing suddenly become a missile hazard during flight. Also, I hate the idea of perfectly good tech taking unnecessary damage.

After all, I'm supposed to be the helpful, good guy, right? Yeah, I'm really just looking out after my own ass. Sue me.

It becomes glaringly obvious that the pilots have no real regard for human or superhuman life as they treat this cargo helicopter like it is a damn Apache.

Terrifying minutes pass as we cut through the air. I can only hazard a guess that we're flying near street level. With every abrupt direction change, my heart plummets slightly and I fight back the desire to blow chunks. This sucks way more than riding those stupid hoversleds. I guess I really don't care for rides in a low-flying helicopter executing vicious turns with no way to tell whether it's just a precaution or whether we are under attack. Call me crazy.

Babe looks like he's going to toss his cookies any second, and Jeannie has already gone to the barf bag once. There really isn't any good choice for me to look at, so I try and close my eyes, which leaves me unprepared for when the Mangler seated to my right cuts loose.

The sound and the smell assault me, and I last maybe ten seconds before I'm scrabbling for my own little baggie and joining Club Ralph.

And to think, my day started off so nicely. The chocolate chip pancakes and breakfast sausages were great, but not so much the second time around. I don't think I'll be having them again for a few weeks.

At this point, even the medic loses her own battle.

"Good thing nobody ran through one of those all-you-can-eat buffets," I mutter.

The blue ox gives me a tired-looking smile. "I just can't wait to get paid and maybe swing back by this way and find that little ranch by the border."

I nod, but say, "Heard some shit went down that way recently. Might not be a good idea. There's even a rumor that the Feds had someone on staff, and a couple of agents died during a raid."

Bobby owns part of that brothel, though the majority owner probably isn't very fond of him right now considering he robbed her and killed a few agents on the grounds.

"Really? Aw, man! This is why we can't have nice things!"

"Cry me a river there, Rocky Mountain Oysters," Jeannie interrupts. "Must be your first time working for the General. She always puts her bases into lockdown for at least seventy-two hours after an op. You ain't going nowhere. So if you are really looking for some action, you might want to ask your lizard buddy if he takes it up the ass."

Figuratively, all the time. Literally? Nope. Man! Talk about seeing a different side to She-Clops.

At least ten more minutes pass before the chopper levels out and flies normally. One of the guards gets a can of air freshener and makes several passes through the cargo area, so the place can smell like lilac-scented vomit. Meanwhile, I make a mental note to get the pilot's name. If possible, I'd like to kill him or her. If not, I want to hire them and use this as an interrogation technique in the future.

They let us off and we're directed into a hangar. It has to be the Mexico site. There is no way we flew long enough to get that far south, even with those crazy-ass pilots. I have Omar's suit over my shoulder and am holding the back-end of the body board. Babe is nice enough, I suppose, to help. We double time it and cut in front of several others to the elevator. This has the benefit of getting me inside the base ahead of the rest.

Yay, me!

By this point, I've finalized my plan. I'm going to play the concerned friend, ask for some lab space where I can work on VZ's suit, activate my tracking device, and hole up until Andy brings my suit to get me the hell of here.

I try not to think about what could possibly go wrong.

Dammit! Jinxed myself.

We descend for perhaps twenty seconds and the door opens up, revealing a waiting medical team. Babe and I follow the instructions and get Omar and the board onto the gurney. The medic calls out his injuries and I follow as closely as I'm allowed.

They wheel him into the OR, and the medic stops me. "This is where we stop. We don't really have a waiting room here, either. I don't want you to get your hopes up. Your friend is in very bad shape and even if they do save him, it will probably be a long time before he can wear his armor again."

"I understand. I'll just have to pray for their success."

Actually, it would be better for me if they don't, but I can't exactly say that to her.

"As will I. Why don't you head down to the debriefing rooms and I'll try and find you if there's any news about your friend. I didn't catch your name."

She's surprisingly nice for a person who works for a boss-level villain, especially given the nasty treatment most Manglers get.

"Matt Harrell, and thanks," I say. "But I'd rather find a lab where I can try and patch Omar's armor up. He'll be asking about it the moment he wakes up."

The woman nods. "Go down three more floors. Those are where the machine shops are. I hope your friend makes it. If you need to find me, ask for Nurse Sharper."

"I appreciate it. Thanks for looking past the skin, too."

She smiles and I wonder if she's a true "animal lover." If she is, she'd be really disappointed by Little Winky.

"No problem. My brother and my cousin did the transformation. Paulo made it, but Vinnie didn't. The money helped pay for my nursing degree. Plus, there seems to be a lot of you guys around here lately."

I'm genuinely grateful. Her last sentence tells me pretty much everything I need to know. Odds are that José is here.

I shuffle off toward the elevators and take a trip down to the machine shop level. There, I make it until I fake it. One thing I've learned about being at a villain's hideout is act like you belong, so I just hiss at one of the techs and tell him I need a spot to work on the armor while ordering him to grab a spool of synthmuscle, a manual winder, and a diagnostics cart.

The man in the lab coat points three doors down and tells me he'll grab what I need. The room is about what I expect from a run-of-the-mill workshop. It's certainly not up to *my* standards or anything like that, but I'll manage. Most importantly, I can now reach into the pouch on the back of my force field vest and . . . feel the tiny pieces of my pulverized GPS tracker with two of my claws.

When did I take a hit hard enough to do that? Shit, Crenshaw's energy spear! Once again jacked over by Athena! Son of a bitch! They won't know which location I'm at! Of course, depending on how far down I am, the signal might be blocked or even jammed.

This day just keeps getting worse. I'm a damn technohermit for a reason!

I'm still fuming internally when the tech arrives with a diagnostics cart and the rest of the material I asked for. He offers to stay and help, but I tell him that I'll call if I need him. I might, actually—these claws are not exactly suited for human-sized tools. I'd be tempted to turn back, but I'm willing to bet there is at least one camera in here and fiddling with it would show that I'm up to no good. So I act like someone trying to fix a powersuit.

It's the role I was born to play.

Thirty minutes pass and I'm starting to get hungry when Gina opens the door. She looks rather downcast. "I've got good news and bad news. Your friend survived the first operations, but I don't want you to get your hopes up. The doctors wanted me to tell you that there was serious bleeding in the brain and things don't look good. Even if you'd gotten off the helicopter and run to the nearest hospital, he'd probably be in just as bad condition."

"And I'd be in jail. Thank you for taking the time to tell me," I say, feeling only slightly sad for the current condition of Omar What's-his-last-name-anyway.

"Would you like to talk about it?"

"No, but if you could get me some food and bring it here, I would be thankful."

"Of course." She points to the table. "You know you don't have to . . ."

Time to lay it on thick. "Yes, yes, I think I do. I will fix his armor, and if I can't find someone worthy to wear it, then I will wear it for him. Besides, I'm guessing all this medical care ain't cheap. When he gets back on his feet, he's going to need cash."

"He must be a good man to deserve your loyalty, Matt. I'll go to the cafeteria and bring you back something."

She leaves and I consider the irony of this good news. Hopefully, word will spread and the people will leave "Velocizapper's concerned Manglermal friend" alone. I can only guess that somewhere between forty-eight hours and one week, my team and Stacy's will launch dual assaults on the two locations. Hopefully, I'm actually at the one where she shows up. My gut says not to even bother creating a new transmitter. The base is too far underground for the signal to carry, and something tells me that there are people in the base just watching for any stray signals."

For the first time in a long time, I'm on my own. I'm stuck in an enemy base, hoping that my lies will continue to mask the truth.

That's not a good thing. If Devious is here, my lies might go up in flames pretty quick. No pressure there whatsoever.

But I'm also Calvin Matthew Stringel, in a workshop with a set of armor and enough tech that I can remake it in my own image.

Time to prove that I can still work my mojo without pieces of a magic teleportation mirror.

I like a good challenge. *Bring it on!*

Chapter Nine

Shoplifting from the Company Store

"Matt, I brought this like you asked," Nurse Gina Sharper says, using the fake name I'd given her, and sets the bag on the table. "It's kind of a mess."

"It's fine. You and the others were trying to save his life," I say. Squatting, I slice the bag open and dump the bloody control suit onto the workbench. The blood didn't bother me nearly as much as the severed bits of circuitry. My claws aren't really designed for the kind of delicate work of rewiring this harness entails, but I'll have to make do.

The harness didn't hurt anyone. Why did it have to suffer?

The Velocizapper suit doesn't use a Direct Neural Interface. Considering how much Omar spent on synthmuscle, I can see why. With enough time, I can correct that, but for now I need to stick with the simplistic kinetic feedback harness Omar created. It has a straightforward simplicity. A quick wrist movement activates and shuts off the plasma ball launchers. The gauntlets won't work in my hybrid form. They'll have to go. Glancing at the clock, I realize I've been in here for almost ten hours. Now that I have the control suit, I can see how hard it's going to be to power this beast up.

Spreading the suit flat on the table, I look at the electrical carnage. "How's Omar doing today?"

"Still no change, I'm afraid. The doctors are taking the fact that he survived the night as a good sign. That is the only good news I have to offer."

"I'll take what I can get, Gina. Thank you." My reply slaps a fresh coat on my current lie. Omar's life or death doesn't really matter to me. Frankly, the world's probably a better place without him in it. Fixing the suit and getting it to where I can use it is far more important in the grand scheme of things.

Fake it until I make it!

Gina doesn't need to know that. She's been nice to me, even if she is a minion of General Devious. It's a stark reminder that not everyone who signs up for a job at a supervillain base is a complete and utter asshole. Even so, there was no need to drop my guard around her. Nurse or not, she'd flip on me at the first sign of trouble. My thoughts flit back to Vicky and how she died in the Overlord's base so many years ago. Having an underling of a top-shelf supervillain giving me the time of day digs up specters from my past.

Maybe I can warn Gina to get out of here while she still can.

Too risky. She'll have to hunker down when things go all stupid.

Face it—Vicky is dead, and I hope Gina can avoid that same fate when the cavalry arrives.

Assuming the cavalry does actually arrive.

The nurse looks up and down the Velicozapper suit and breaks me out of my moment of contemplation. "You're making changes."

"You said it yourself. Even if Omar pulls out of this, he's not going to be suiting up anytime soon. I might as well fix it for me and use it to pull some jobs so that he can build a new suit from scratch with the money I bring in. Instead of hand actuators, I'm replacing them with claws. Fine motor skill will suffer, but the two claws should compensate for it."

It also gives me the chance to try and mess with those powerclaws that Cuban superheroine, Honey Badger, uses. It's an easy upgrade— a speed suit that has claws that can cut through most anything. It makes more sense than just tossing plasma balls around. Omar usually avoids direct combat, probably out of fear that his delicate suit would end up— well, like this. He'd circle around people, lobbing plasma at them. Naturally, I'm keeping the plasma launchers; they help cool the suit, and weigh far less than any heat exchangers I could install. With more time, I'll try to find the right spot for a sonic generator and once more rip off The Biloxi Bugler. But that idea is on the back burner in favor of getting the suit up and running and me inside of it.

It's the challenge, I realize. With Mega, I can have anything and everything I ever wanted without any power or space limitations—like playing all those first-person shooters back at the base in God mode, unlimited ammo and impregnable shields. Now, I am looking for every square inch of space where I can fit something and every spare kilogram of weight.

I miss this game and the thrill of getting something done despite the problems surrounding me.

"Have you been debriefed yet?"

To lie or not to lie? "No. What's the point? I ran around, caused a little chaos and then had to drag my pal's limp form back to the chopper. I get it, I'm a grunt . . . a small little gecko, I guess, out running with the big lizards."

"You should go," she says. "Everyone gets debriefed and you know that. I've already been. There's only a couple of people left in line."

"Seriously," I lisp the "s" with my slightly misshapen tongue.

The nurse gives me an exasperated look and says, "Matt, I'm just looking out for you. If they come looking for you, you won't like it. They'll have someone stronger than you drag your ass down there."

"I'll go as soon as I get this harness cleaned up. Promise."

She takes me at my word and wishes me a good evening. I start swabbing at the bloodstains with some wipes as I inspect the damaged circuits. The doctors must have used some shears to split the material. I'll need at least a day, maybe two given the fact that I have to use my claws, to reconnect those breaks and try to add some room. Omar has a runner's build, and in my human form I have a "run to the fridge and grab something to eat" build. My hybrid body needs even more space. With the stubby tail, I've got "junk in the trunk," which will require further modifications.

Thirty minutes pass and I realize that time isn't on my side. The claws aren't up for delicate work, and I don't dare revert to being human. I need something different. Why not some weak magic instead? Concentrating on a simple levitation spell, the one I used to impress Stacy when she got her memories back, I float the ends of the wires back together and use the soldering iron taped to my right claw to join them.

Success! The spell takes very little to maintain with some good old cold blood running through my veins.

Now just a couple of thousand more to go.

Better go down and debrief. It's been a full hour since Gina left and she probably told them about me, so I'd better go and play insignificant Manglermal. Maybe I can get an idea where José is being held.

Unplugging the soldering iron, I peel away the tape and set it aside. The control suit is still a wreck, but almost all of the blood is gone and I will be able to make it work . . . eventually.

"Better go down to the rooms and report in," I say, more for anyone who might be monitoring the room.

• • •

"You look like crap! Where've you been?" Babe the blue-ish ox asked. He and two other Manglers are all that are left, waiting to be seen.

"Trying to find out how my partner was doing and seeing if I can salvage his suit. Plus, I figured everyone else would cut in front of us anyway . . . just because."

Babe and the hammerhead shark lady next to him, with a breathing device connected to her gills, nod at my assessment.

As I'd implied to the nurse, Manglers are way down on the pecking order, just a hair above regular grunt soldiers. They're considered less than human, mostly extra muscle who are faster, stronger, and have better reflexes than a normal person. As strong as Babe might be, Bobby would beat the snot out of him, and my buddy is only a few rungs up the ladder.

Then again, Bobby did give his Gulf Coast Guardian cousin a serious smackdown when they fought in New Orleans, so he might be climbing out of the C-List category.

"How about you?" I ask. "I'm sure you weren't waiting in line all this time."

"I ate, grabbed some rack time and went down to the bottom level to pay my respects to Doc Mangler."

The mention of Doc Mangler confirms that my captured friend is here. Manglers, in general, give their deranged creator way too much hero worship, but I know better than to say anything to contradict their opinions. Who knows? It might be coded into their genetics. The Doctor is a figure revered by almost every one of his creations. Some don't care for him. Like the few Mangler heroes, or someone like Anemone who isn't really a hero, but is still with the Gulf Coasters for some odd reason.

From what I know about Sanford Marley Acojo, he probably likes the paycheck, and since his power merely paralyzes people, the Gulf Coast Guardians let him do it without restraint.

As far as Doc Mangler is concerned, I'm not completely sold on the asshole's omnipotence. He's the son of a Nazi scientist that the Russians gave sanctuary to after World War II. They got what they deserved in the end. The people protecting him and his father and keeping the two of them off everyone's radar became the very first Manglermals.

The rest is history, littered with the bodies of failed experiments and the victims of the successful transformations, like the ones I am standing next to.

"I should go down and see him," I state.

"You haven't already?" the hammer head asks, sounding like a nosy suburban housewife who just discovered a scandal in the cul-de-sac. Her eyes, so far apart like that, creep me out.

I shrug and shake my head, deciding to shut up and let the others draw their own conclusions from my silence.

"You shouldn't be embarrassed," Babe says. "Be different. Be proud."

Imagining all the shit Bobby would give me if he was here right now, I say, "I am. It's just been a long day and I'm burnt out. This place might feel OK to normal, but it's too cold for me. I'd prefer it to be another ten or fifteen degrees warmer."

"Way, way too dry for me," the shark woman adds in agreement. "As soon as we get out of here, I'm going for a long swim."

The penguin guy or girl at the front of our little line grunts.

One of the rooms opens up and a Mangler walks out, a male gypsy moth. I recognize him from my stint in prison—a small time thief. Of course they could say the same thing about me, back in the day. The penguin waddles away and into the open room.

Eventually, my turn comes. The room is small, designed to make someone feel uncomfortable. The tiny, confining chair won't work with my frame, so I'm forced to stand in front of one of Devious's goonsquad.

"I don't have you down on our list. Mr. Harrell, is it?"

"Look under Bad Raptor," I offer. "If it isn't under that, then shit . . . I dunno."

I'd think about saying more, offering up some kind of human input error or something, but don't want to sound like I'm trying to lead him. Instead, I'm banking on my interrogator's long-ass day making him sloppy.

"Not there, either," the interviewer growls and massages his bald head.

"Figures," I mutter. "Shit like that always seems to happen to me! Do you guys always have computer problems like this?"

OK, maybe a little steering is in order.

"There's a high turnover in the IT group," the man says. "My damn access token doesn't work half the time and then they're always having an outage for something. If they're not patching the databases, they're patching the workstations, or the portal is down. It's a fucking nightmare. I figure if someone's got the stones to hack into our system, we'll just kill them when we find out who they are."

"Sounds rough," I say sympathetically. Lucky for me, I have a "no shit" artificial intelligence to take care of all my computing needs and not a very big network, either. Before Andy, I'd done the computer work, and I thought Bobby was going to take a swing at me when our new firewall blocked around eighty percent of all the porn sites.

"You should try typing with these," I say and wave a clawed hand in the air. "I feel you, though. Back at my house, I tried setting up the speech to text program. With my lisp, that was a waste of time!" I play the confidence game and try to help my cause by giving my interviewer an easy scapegoat.

"Let me pull up the portal and see if I can get one of the DBAs to see if they can find your record," the man says.

"Really isn't much to tell . . . I was causing a little havoc and then stumbled onto Velocizapper, that Twin Taser woman, and freed them. VZ and I tried to cut down an alley and ran into one of the damn Olympians—the bitch with spears. She jacked up VZ really bad and I had to lose her before I could circle back and get him. After that, it was just about carrying VZ to a chopper and getting him looked at. Didn't even get a chance to do any smash and grabs."

The guy looks up from his screen. "The DBAs are on a meal break, I got the automated submit a ticket crap. Let me just get a pad of paper and I'll write it down."

"Sounds good to me."

Patiently, I wait for him to get the necessary tools for an interview and then repeat my half-truths for him. It is all very low-key. That's the problem with trying to become a major villain; if your organization gets too big, you get too big. You end up hiring people, and unless you luck out and get someone like Vicky, they become your weakest link.

Bobby and I used to joke that having to hire a support staff was what kept us from starting a top tier crime syndicate—that and talent.

Hell! My time with the Coasters left a bad taste in my mouth for having a bunch of employees. I'll stick with Andy every day of the week!

Thankfully, the guy is just half-assing it anyway. For all he knows, I'm just a filthy Manglermal, a super-powered nobody. In less than ten minutes, I'm out of there after listing what supers I'd seen and what I'd seen them do.

After leaving the room, I walk to one of the elevators and go down two more levels to where the cafeteria is. Since I'm out and about, I might as well take in the sights. Until I finish the modifications to the VZ armor, I don't plan on visiting Mangler. Plus, I'll probably do something stupid the moment I see José. Even with a new suit, I'll still be a little under gunned against the people running around this place.

I can freely admit to a slight case of "base envy." My setup is . . . somewhat lacking, in comparison to this beast. If I could stand the heat of Mexico, I'd be sorely tempted to capture this place and move our operations here. Whereas I have two and a half levels sixty feet under Alabama, Devious has eight levels with each of them roughly the size of a big-box retail store. It's almost like a damn inverted skyscraper.

And this isn't even her main base!

Even so, it doesn't match up to the Overlord's Omega base.

Passing through the automated cafeteria line, I don't get any looks from the repurposed Type-A robot serving as a mechanical lunch lady. I can see another one in the kitchen area with extra arm upgrade attachments. For a techie like myself, that just seems gratuitous, like Devious is flaunting.

What next? Type-B robots with room service trays attached to their gyroscopic forms?

• • •

Much to my surprise, a pair of techs are fiddling around with the VZ armor when I return to the workshop. "Just what the hell do you two think you're doing?"

The taller one looks up from the laptop he has connected into the head assembly. "Orders, jackass. We're pulling the video footage. Someone told someone else that this pile of scrap ran into Megasuit. Praetorius told our supervisor who told us. If you got a problem with it, lizardman, by all means take it up with Praetorius."

When I don't say anything, the guy looks back down and mutters, "Yeah, thought so."

The Italian strongman is known to throw down with Ares. His presence here complicates things. Even with Mega, I wouldn't want to be stuck in a confined space with him.

"Cut him some slack, Bryce," the older, shorter, white-haired tech says.

"Maybe he shouldn't come walking in like he owns the place and asking us what the hell we're doing. Last I checked, this is one of our workshops and he's the visitor."

"Sorry, just finished getting debriefed and eating some meat that I couldn't identify. Relax!"

"He's always like that," the more pleasant one says. I'm Dean."

Waving a claw at him, I reply, "I'm Matt. How much longer do you think you'll be? I've gotta get back to patching this thing up."

"Shouldn't be but another ten or fifteen minutes. If you'd been here, we'd already be done. Took us almost twenty minutes to find the access port in the head gear."

I shrug, not wanting to admit that I wouldn't have known where the access port is either. That would not have gone well for my cover.

Bryce sticks to his work while Dean becomes my new best friend. He handles this level's supply and inventory. I ask him where I can get a bunch of things and he taps away on his handheld. Moments later, he starts calling out locations. My piss-poor writing skills aren't needed because he prints it out for me.

I'm liking Dean more and more. Bryce is still giving me the occasional dirty look—which translates into us not getting along very well.

Surprisingly, I'm OK with that. Besides, I think I can talk Dean into staying to help me with some of the more detailed work that my dinosaur claws aren't really suited for.

"So did you actually see the Megasuit?" Dean asks.

"Only briefly," I say. "There was one of the female Olympians and someone else there. They were a little out of my league."

Dean nods in an understanding fashion, while Bryce does as well, but in a more condescending manner.

Just can't catch a break with this one, can I?

It's not like I'm really interested in befriending either of these two. I just need to keep them mostly out of my hair until VZ is up and running. My mind starts searching for ways to slow down Praetorius. The few times I threw down with Ares hadn't exactly been resounding victories for team Mechani-Cal. I overloaded and blew up a weapon in his face, which knocked him on his ass long enough for me to run away as fast as I could. The other time was when I made a "last stand" on the steps of Mount Olympus. Ares was part of the group of mind-controlled heroes who overran my position.

Not one of my best memories, even if it all worked out in the end.

• • •

Two days later, the new armor is beginning to take shape. It still has some of the slim lines Omar designed, but it now looks a tad more menacing and more reptilian in appearance. The leg joints are reversible, so I can use it in both my hybrid and human forms. One of the things I have to actively fight is my desire to load this thing down with weaponry. Once I can get the portal shards into it, I can give it the overhaul that it deserves. Until then, be fast and vent plasma balls all over the place.

"If it isn't my favorite Techno-Mal. How's it going?" Dean asks, gawking at the suit suspended from a pair of chain falls, with the legs cycling at full speed. Assuming he's been keeping tabs from the cameras, he already has a good idea.

"The damage is repaired and the mods have been installed. I'm testing the patch job you did on the control harness. Thanks for all that delicate work, by the way."

"Is it holding up?"

"Seems to, at least at speed," I say and let the legs spin down. "Below ten miles per hour, it has these glitches that I can't seem to isolate—spasms. Eventually, I'll have to build a replacement harness, but if I had to use it now it would work. Trying to stand still would make me look like a drunken sailor. Might not even be damage. It might me some kind of feedback loop considering it was designed for a pure human."

"Already planning some jobs when you get out of here?"

I nod and flick my tongue. "You could say that."

"Good. You do realize, I wasn't allowed to just *give* you the repair parts. You're going to be in the General's pocket until you pay off your debt. We aren't running a charity here."

At least I am expecting this—the old company store hustle. Villainous organizations don't do favors and there are no free lunches. Hell, they're probably deducting the meals and any extras from all the hired help's paydays. For the tech types, there's the workshops. The other half of the cafeteria level houses a mini-mall, bar, and brothel. The week-long "debriefing" is to ensure no one betrays the operation and also gives General Devious the opportunity to reduce the amount she's actually paying.

"Yeah, I realized you were the good cop and Bryce was the bad cop pretty quickly. Are they looking for money or servitude? More importantly, how much extra will it run me for enough tech to wire a replacement harness instead of counting on this?"

Might as well fish for some extra tech. I can do without a suit that's prone to seizures at low speed. It's not like I'm going to be repaying them, either.

Dean smiles and looks relieved. "Oh, good. I was worried I'd have to explain how things work to you. Beats me, I'm the nice one, remember? Bryce is the one you'll have to negotiate with, but I'd take whatever he offers you. It'll likely be the best one you get."

People like Nurse Sharper are still the exception and not the rule. Even this Dean fellow, or Bryce . . . no, scratch that! Bryce is probably still a tool. Anyway, even Dean might be an OK guy out in the real world.

This is about as far as you can get from the real world.

Hell! For all I know, Gina is probably in on it too, and some bean counter is probably up there adding the cost of Omar's medical care to my account. That's one of the many downsides to the supervillain lifestyle—the healthcare plans usually blows chunks.

If I am a betting human/dinosaur hybrid, I'm guessing my missions would involve just enough damage to the suit to keep lil' old Matt Harrell indentured to General Devious's Company Store until the cows came home.

"I'll be happy to speak with Bryce about the necessary arrangements. Why don't you go ahead and start pulling together the material I'll need for a new harness, while we hammer out the details?"

A few seconds later, Bryce walks in. "Glad to hear you'll be joining us, Matt. Dean, grab the stuff for a new harness, and also we'll be needing a sprayer attachment and a two gallon cylinder to mount on the back of the suit. Praetorius has a job for you, Mr. Harrell."

Chapter Ten

The Many Deaths of José Six-Pack

Bryce leads me toward the south end of the level and calls the elevator. Dean is busy getting all the components I'll need for the new control harness, along with the sprayer attachment. Since it looks like I am starting a tab with the company store, I might as well abuse it.

My concern about a weaponized form of the Manglermal process grows. It's not too terribly hard to put a speed suit, a delivery mechanism, and Doctor Igor Mangelov together to come up with a very nasty idea. They can probably even simplify the process with a drone like my floater design—Targeted Manglerification. Do what we want or we'll turn you into a hideous monster. Bow down or we'll take away your humanity.

If I removed the weaponry from the floater design and installed a noise cancellation system, it would be completely quiet, low profile, and half the size.

Bad Cal! Stop trying to improve a really heinous idea!

General Devious must be proud of this one. I'm guessing she almost wishes Patterson were still among the living. Destroying Ultraweapon's pretty-boy good looks and humanity would have been something she'd do in a heartbeat.

Me? I'm just happy that shithead is dead, and if I get the opportunity, the good General will join him. Her telepathy and telekinesis make her deadly enough, although I cling to the belief that The Overlord is the greater threat—probably because he has to work harder at it. Who knows what that bastard is up to right now?

"So why'd you go through with it?" Bryce asks as we enter the lift.

"Huh?"

"Go Mangler," he replies.

"Money," I answer him with something he would expect. "Or the distinct lack of money, to be more precise."

"Was it worth it?"

"Why? Thinking of going native?"

"I'm hearing the new formula is over ninety percent effective."

"That's still ten percent fatal," I comment. "If you ever played Dungeons and Dragons, that twenty-sided dice would roll a one at the worst of times." *Talk about the ultimate Critical Fail!*

"Yeah, yeah. But I really want to know if it's worth it?"

I need a more straightforward answer. I pause for a moment to get it right. "Depends on if you like hurting people by making something with your brains and your hands, or if you just want to skip the whole making part and go straight to the hurting people. Your hands will get a lot dirtier this way. If you don't like the way your voice sounds and want a change, it might be for you. If you're not a fan of fine dining, you don't have to worry about getting seated at just about any restaurant, and the dating life sucks ass unless you're into other Manglers."

Or are Bobby. Dude's into some freaky shit, I add in my head.

Even at the lowest point in my life, working in that run-down auto shop after being blackballed from everything resembling a tech job by Patterson's legal vultures, I hadn't considered becoming a Manglermal. I can already attest to how hard it is to work on a set of armor with claws instead of fingers. Besides, I mostly believe Stacy when she says that she doesn't care about my "average" looks, but given how unimpressed she is with my hybrid form, I doubt she'd like it if the change became permanent.

The elevator comes to a halt, but the door does not open. I try to mask my anxiety as the human next to me pushes the call button three times and waves to the camera dome. The floor shudders and we descend one more level.

My previous case of base envy pops the clutch and goes into overdrive. *A huge base with a bonus hidden level? Shit! I am totally going to steal this place one day!*

I suppose if I am dreaming big, I'd want Mount Olympus. But to be perfectly honest, the manmade Mountain in Northern Virginia is a *government facility* with everything that entails—rows and rows of cubicles filled with bureaucrats who endlessly schedule meetings and use the words "metrics" and "process improvement" like it is the gospel. I'd rather have a colon cleansing.

Even this place has its own brand of red tape, but I can deal with it. I wonder if Stacy will help me conquer this place.

• • •

My former teammate is stuck in a three-chamber plastic cell, reminding me of that bubble boy movie. An airlock separates the two ends. José sits glumly on a cot, staring daggers at all of us. He looks disheveled and run down. It sucks that I'm not in a position to do anything about it right now. Until I case the layout, it's recon over rescue. I can't afford to go "hero stupid" right now.

I can't really spare him much more than a glance right now. I have my own problems staring me in the face.

"You don't look like one of my children." The voice belongs to Doctor Igor Mangelov. He's the son of a German war criminal scientist and his Russian handler. The White Rhino is leaning up against a table looking bored while Praetorius is inspecting the machinery.

The part of the room consisting of José's cell and the adjacent part look perfectly clinical, everything one would expect from a confinement unit. The rest, however, gives the appearance of a mad scientist's laboratory . . . a very, very mad scientist. Apparently, the good doctor doesn't care much for a janitorial staff, or maybe he ended up experimenting on them. My guess is the latter.

"I'm not," I reply with a dismissive wave of my ill-formed appendage. "It's really a magical accident. It's easier to let them think I'm a Manglermal. Actually, he was there."

My longest claw points at José. I figure I can try and clue him in that there is more going on, if he's paying close attention.

"Go on," the old scientist says.

"I drove a delivery route in Louisiana a couple of years back. Some dinosaur sonuvabitch starts turning everyone into lizards. The Gulf Coasters stopped him, and fixed pretty much everyone else but me."

José stares at me and I see the curious expression in his eyes. In the aftermath of the battle with Tyrannosorcerer Rex, She-Dozer made certain to brief the team on at least three occasions that everyone had been fixed. He should know I'm lying.

Walking to the cell, I look at him. "I never thought I would see him again. Hopefully he gets what's coming to him. So yeah, byproduct of a magical accident—that's me."

I'm tempted to wink at him, but who knows where the cameras are situated, or even what a wink in my current form would look like. After the first few transformations, I never stood and watched my reflection.

Rhino's deep, gravelly voice interrupts my staring contest with my teammate. "If he is not one of us, we should put someone else in the suit."

"You're not doing anything with my suit without me."

"It's not your suit to begin with," Rhino dismisses my complaint. "Plus, I don't trust him."

"You can trust I will take your money to do the job, but we're not exactly the Boy Scouts here."

"My friend has a point, Mr. Harrell," Doctor Mangler adds. "You may very well be susceptible to my newest formula."

"I'll make sure the suit is buttoned up tight. Besides, unless you've got another one of your children around with the same body type as me, you'll lose several days while the suit needs to be adjusted. Then you'll lose several more while someone learns how to run the suit. So if you want to go that route, I'm cool. You'll have to pay me to rig the suit for someone else and then you'll pay me again to teach that dumbshit how to run it. Omar isn't exactly up for playing teacher right now. Either way, I'll get paid."

"You're a smug little gecko. I bet I could just stomp you into a bloody smear on the ground. Your little claws won't get through my hide."

"And how exactly would that help get your job done?" I hold my hand up and make it shimmer. "There's a bit more to me than a claw. Magical accident, remember?"

Rhino glowers at me, but when he takes a step forward Praetorius reaches out and puts his hand on the Mangler, stopping him. "Not here."

That's not exactly a ringing endorsement. I don't really know if the single mage bolt I could conjure would do anything other than knock him on his ass. Sadly, it would knock me on my ass too, but I don't offer that. That's the problem with having more determination than actual talent with magic. Right about now, I could use a plasma cannon or two.

"So since we're not going to throw down, what's the actual job and how much is it going to make me? More importantly, is this going to wipe the slate clean with your company store?"

"It will clear some of the debt," Praetorius answers smoothly.

"Let's hear about the job and then agree on the price."

"There is some risk," Doc Mangler interrupts. "Since you are not really one of my children, there is a chance the agent could very well affect you."

This ought to be interesting. "Like I said before, the suit can be airtight before the end of the day."

"Very well then. Continue on, Massimo."

Praetorius nods. "We need to test the newest agent in the field. The speedsuit is a suitable delivery vehicle that we can take advantage of."

"Anything specific in mind?"

Mangler answers this time. "Would you be surprised to know that this is effective against even some people with powers?"

Now that is a new one! "I have always heard that people with powers are immune to your process."

"Ah, but sometimes when we research and experiment there is a breakthrough! And I believe that this will be the one that rewrites civilization as we know it. Since we're out of willing test subjects, it's time to find some unwilling ones."

"Who do you have in mind?" It makes me wonder where they got *willing* test subjects from.

Praetorius takes over. "Spiritstaff and his wife K-Otica for starters. The man is magically protected through his weapon, and the woman's power levels fluctuate radically. At speed, you should be able to dose them and be gone before they can react."

"For the right price, I think I can do that," I say, realizing that it's time to get to the negotiation phase. Nothing like dusting off my old villain thinking cap to do some old-fashioned haggling. "The op sounds straightforward, but I'm worried about the fallout. I could give a shit about the man. Hell, I've always thought he was an asshole. K-Otica is a whole different story. Even if I catch the woman when she isn't near her peak, she's very popular down this way and in the States, too. Making her into an abomination could very easily get me a price on my head and heroes chasing me to the ends of the Earth. Writing off my balance sheet ain't gonna cut that shit, if you hear what I'm saying?"

Ding! A timer goes off from a nearby workbench. Doctor Mangler hobbles over to it and resets it. "Our negotiations must wait for a brief period."

He points to the prisoner. "It is time for another test subject, if you please. Come now, my friend. I thought we were beyond this game of refusals and threats."

José appears even less happy than when I first arrived, if that is possible. He mouths several curses and takes off his shirt. I've watched him spawn a clone before back in our days in New Orleans. It's one of those spectacles that is so gross that you can't help but stare. He downs a trio of carb-loaded shakes and braces himself. On the left side of his back a boil begins to form and rapidly swell like a balloon.

Turn away Cal; you don't need to watch this! Turn the hell away.

But like an idiot, I don't, and the boil reaches the size of a beach ball before it detaches from the back of my friend. The prime version of José stumbles back onto the bed and pulls a plastic sheet up. Within moments, the fleshy sack doubles in size and bursts open, splattering blood and puss all over the reinforced, transparent walls. In the aftermath, a goo-covered copy of José stands and twists himself back and forth for a good ten seconds, uncaring about the fact that he is naked.

I remember joking with José that if they forced high school Sex Ed classes to watch him make a clone, the number of teenage pregnancies would drop like a rock.

I might have even offered to record it, and set up the distribution as well. But like many of my money making schemes, it didn't pan out. Things were simpler back then.

"Experiment number three seven two," Mangler speaks into his tablet. Pushing a button, he releases the door to the attached airlock room. He then waves to José to send his freshly spawned counterpart into the smaller room.

I cringe, realizing how many of his clones have gone through the procedure, and I know for a fact that José feels the feedback each time one of his duplicates is killed.

"Test subject will be exposed to twenty-five milliliters of enhanced protocol Four Nine Seven Three Lima, delivered by aerosol. Current success rate with this protocol has been ninety-three point four percent. Subject will be exposed to sixty different images of a jaguar at a rate of one per second for one minute before the agent is released, and for two additional minutes post-release in our ongoing attempt to steer the transformation. In addition, the scent of a male jaguar will also be released into the transformation chamber along with audio recordings."

Targeted Manglermal transformations? He's tried that in the past, but has never really gotten it to work. Let's hope he isn't any closer to getting that! Just the fact that he has a ninety-three percent success rate should frighten most people. I guess he's satisfied that about seven percent don't survive the process. At nearly four hundred experiments, poor José has had to experience almost thirty transformation deaths. I've heard those are horrible! Then again, even the ones that survive the treatment and become Manglers are killed shortly afterward. He feels each of those, too! He may be on the verge of going insane.

The clone walks with his head held high into the small booth and watches as the door back into José prime's chamber is sealed. Defiantly, he stares Doc Mangler down and extends both of his middle fingers.

That act alone convinces me that I need to sell Wendy on recruiting José for our team. His talents are clearly being wasted working with the Gulf Coasters. I originally wanted to make cheap knockoffs of my Mark I Mechani-Cal suit for his clones to wear. I could probably do Velocizapper knockoffs for much less. There'd be no flight systems, and that would be a cost savings, but I'd have to weigh it against the increased cost of synthmuscle. One VZ suit wouldn't be a real threat to the mid-listers out there, but five acting in concert might even give the low end of the top tier of supervillains cause for concern.

Of course, my future plans won't help this clone. The animal noises begin as I watch clone José grimace. I can see him actively trying not to look at any of the images and trying to throw off the experiment in his own special way.

Good for him! Stick it to the man!

As the animal noises grow more intense, I witness Doc Mangler switching on the rest of his gear. The clone covers his mouth with his hand, but I don't expect that it will do any more than give him a few extra seconds of protection. Or maybe not, if this new crap is absorbed through the skin.

Seconds pass and then suddenly, clone José's screams join the animal noises as he collapses to the ground and begins writhing in pain. I spare a glance over to the real José and see my friend is suffering from the feedback.

Yeah, I'm pretty much an asshole, but even assholes don't like to watch people they like in pain. This is a shitty situation all around.

Time passes. It feels like something along the lines of five minutes, but I suspect that it is really around two. The José on the ground is now covered in brown fur, complete with long ears and white fur markings all along his ass.

The clone has turned into, and I shit you not, Peter Cottontail. The common rabbit is a far cry from a fierce jaguar.

Mangler moves closer to the sealed booth and activates his recorder. "Experiment Three Seven Two survived the transformation, but did not turn into a jaguar as I had hoped. This continues the trend of seeing a lower rate of success with the directed transformations from the clone over the results of the volunteers. My suspicions are that the subject's familiarity with the process and the accompanying pain trigger the fear instinct with the resulting transformation becoming not the jaguar, but the prey of the jaguar. I will compensate by dosing the donor with mood-enhancement drugs to see if a lessened fear and anxiety level will improve our success rate. Sedating the test subject is also a possibility."

The rabbit hybrid is struggling to get to his feet when Doctor Mangler depresses a button on the tablet he holds. The effect is nauseating. The power flickers and dims as the resulting electrical power is driven into the cage. Even if José had managed to get a body that was stronger, it couldn't have protected him from the electrical current. The end result is a dead rabbitman.

White Rhino laughs as a pair of Type-A robots are summoned. "Wonder if he would taste like chicken? Too bad you can't find something that preys on lemmings and then hit Congress and the White House with it, Doc. Then you could show all the politicians to the nearest cliff."

The robots draw blood samples from the body and then carry it over to a sealed tanning-bed-like coffin, where it's either superheated or irradiated, I can't be sure. Whatever it does, it must kill off any of the remaining agent. Perhaps another minute goes by before the robots bag the whole body and carry it to what looks like an oversized dumbwaiter. I suppress a smile. The dumbwaiter constitutes another way down to this level. I'll have to keep that in mind.

Mangler turns back to me. "Now, back to our discussion concerning your employment, Mr. . . . . Harrell, is it?"

"Correct, sir."

"You and your suit will be in service to me for a period of one year. You will be paid a flat fee of fifty thousand U.S. dollars per month and you will receive a two million U.S. dollar payment at the end of this year period. Unlike the area effect weapons we plan to deploy, you are to be a surgical instrument that will deliver my product to specific individuals."

"Keeping the suit running is going to burn through thirty to forty grand a month, so make it one hundred grand a month and you can lower the bonus at the end to one point five million. Plus, my slate with the base is clean. Wouldn't want to spend a year working for you only for them to come along and tell me that I'm going to do another year for them, right?"

Praetorius gives me an appraising look. "Your current slate will be clean starting now, should you accept the good Doctor's offer. If you succeed, I'll negotiate for your services after you leave his employment. Any charges you run up from this moment on—they are a different matter. If you fail or betray us, I'll personally have you thrown in that booth and we can find out whether the magic that made you is stronger than the science of the Doctor."

The old me would have jumped at that offer. It's probably one of the best offers I've ever gotten in my career as an armored grunt. Too bad I'm not interested in those kinds of jobs nowadays. I try to tap back into the much younger and much stupider Cal Stringel to lie to them one more time.

"I think your deal works. Count me in!"

Chapter Eleven

Why Heroism Can Sometimes Be Like Herpes

"I thought you and the Rhino were seriously going to fight there, Raptorman," Bryce says. "Couldn't quite see how he reacted when you did that magic thing, but I'm pretty sure he reevaluated his position pretty quick. So, why'd you lie to me about being a Mangler?"

"It's the easiest explanation, and it's not like we are bros or anything." The guy almost seems offended that I fed him some bullshit.

Naturally, I want to give him a second helping. That's a heady reminder of what it's really like to be a villain. You can lie as much as you want, not caring one bit.

I sort of miss it.

"So yeah, it was more of a magical accident, and since it's not going to go away without some serious coin and a decent sorcerer or sorceress who is willing to look the other way, that's why I'm working. I heard it through the grapevine that the General has a few medicine men, a fakir, and a couple of bokors on her staff. Maybe if I make enough, I can get one of them to try and cure me."

I have no doubt that tidbit will make its way back to my new employers, but that should make them think they have leverage on me. Besides, once you start lying, it's hard to stop and when needed, my relationship with the truth is more flexible than at least an Olympic bronze medalist in gymnastics.

"If you and White Rhino went at it, who would win?"

"Me," I say without any hesitation. "Why?"

"Without the suit?"

"Also me. Once again, why?"

"Might post it on the betting board and see if I get any takers," he says, sounding cryptic.

"Betting board?"

"Yeah, we place bets on who would win in a fight. Rhino likes to tussle and assert his dominance over the Manglers. You're pretty much an unknown right now, so if I get in on the early action I can get some favorable odds if the two of you fight."

"There's not a lot to do around here, is there?"

"We're paid well, but gotta do something to pass the time. Just picked up four large a couple of weeks ago when my bet on that Stringel guy still being alive paid out."

Now it's my turn to be somewhat offended. "I wouldn't rule out a shapeshifter or a clone. The story sounds fishy to me."

"Yeah, Bragg down in IT didn't want to pay up and says that he wants the money back if it turns out to be a fake, but it's pretty hard to fool a genetic test, so Barry caved and paid out a sweet forty-to-one longshot."

Shrugging, I bare my fangs in what approximates a smile. Personally, I think my own survival should rate a better payout, but I suppose I have a certain amount of bias in this matter.

• • •

"Aw, man! You went to the lowest level?" Dean asks. "I've never been there before. What's it like?"

"Machines, some robots, more machines, and a really pissed-off Gulf Coast Guardian."

Bryce dropped me off after the meeting and I haven't seen him again in the twelve or so hours since. I wonder what odds he got on my potential fight with White Rhino and if I should place a bet on myself out of principle.

Shit! Maybe I'm getting bored, too?

As for Dean, he's been hanging around, apparently with no other task than to keep an eye on me, unless the General doesn't mind slackers on the payroll. If so, I'd like to apply.

I've got the suit sealed and pressurized. For the next fifteen minutes, the reading on the gauge attached to the suit is the only thing I care about, but that doesn't stop Dean recounting his life story to me. It would be nice to start in on Floater Mark II using their equipment, but I don't intend to bite off more than I can chew.

Dean likes to sail. He started when he lived in Rhode Island.

My life is so much better knowing this.

He takes his son out when he gets vacation from here and he has his weekend visitation. He owns a small catamaran berthed in Puerto Vallarta.

That at least gives me an idea of what's within traveling distance, maybe a hundred miles or so of Mexico's Pacific Coast. It also makes me glad that Wendy and I are on decent terms, even though she's never really been my ex. Hell, it doesn't qualify as a friends with benefits. More like two ships passing in the night that spawned a little tugboat nine months later.

"Hello, Matt. Oh. Hey, Dean," Gina says entering the room. "I've got news about Omar."

All those years of being a self-important asshole work against me as I pretend to give a shit about Omar's condition. "What's the latest?"

"They're going to try and ease him out of the medically-induced coma tomorrow. The surgeon said it was touch and go there, but they think he's going to make it."

Hurray for the douchebag! "That's good to hear. Though, I might be gone before he's fully conscious."

Which will be a good thing, I add in my head. *Man! I really want a new drone!*

"I'd heard that you were going to do some jobs for Praetorius," she says. Her eyes flit over to Dean and it seems like she wants to say something more and then decides not to.

Office politics on a supervillain's base must be a bitch of epic proportions.

"Yeah, that's why I'm double checking the suit. The seals have to hold."

"Be careful," she advises. "Word in the halls is that you're not a real Mangler, and who knows what that stuff will do to you?"

Dean doesn't look completely surprised, so I can assume Bryce ran his mouth, probably after getting what he thought were his best odds.

If I really were Matt Harrell, accidental magical lizardman, I'd be angry at this horrid breach of trust!

"I see news travels fast," I say, deciding to sound peeved, but not make a scene over it.

She smiles at me. "If you could run that suit at the speed of gossip around here, you'd be faster than Hermes."

"Wouldn't your telepathic boss have an issue with gossiping?"

Gina adopts a more serious face. "You're still an outsider, fair game and all that. We know not to talk about her business, and we know what happens to those that do. Hang around long enough and you'll have her in your head one day."

"Sounds like a party I wouldn't mind missing." Considering I'd actually had a telepathic conversation with the woman during the HORDES fiasco, it's not something I would care to repeat. I'm fairly certain the last thing I would ever see before she killed me would be the momentary look of surprise on her face, and if I die looking at a woman, I plan on it being Stacy—far in the future, when I am a very, very old man.

• • •

"Get in your suit," Bryce states, shouting over the alarms. "They need you on the lower level!"

I'm already way ahead of him and am over halfway dressed. Sadly, all the progress on my new drone is a couple of really bad concept drawings. My artistic skills are mediocre on the best days. Like most activities that don't involve slashing things, claws seem to get in the way. "What the hell is going on?"

"Even if I knew, I wouldn't tell you. That sprayer attachment ready?"

"As it's ever going to be," I answer. That's not entirely true. I wouldn't mind another three or four operational checks on the sprayer attachment, or the suit in general, but that's the engineer in me talking. Plus with this many alarms, I've got a pretty good idea what's about to happen. My ride is here and as fortune would have it, the bad guys want me to go back down to the guy I'm here to rescue.

I fight the smile trying to form on my face and take a last look around the room I plan to pillage like a modern-day Viking. I know I'll just jinx myself if I start to think this is going to be easy. Once I get José free, I'll still have to go through an entire base worth of villains to get out of here. Or I could hunker down and wait for the cavalry to come rescue us.

It's good to have options. I'm not picky.

"Head for the back elevator," Bryce commands.

Finishing the power-on sequence, I lumber out the door toward the rooms. I can immediately tell that the suit's kinetic power stabilizers are off. Being a step up from a standard human, I'm a bit stronger and faster, and the VZ suit still can't quite compensate for it. My mind starts to determine how I can engineer a fix for this, but I try to push those nervous thoughts aside and press forward. I quickly stumble down the hallway like a giant, metallic drunken toddler. The reversed knees still feel just as odd as when I run in this form. If I had more time, I'd have transformed back into my human form and slipped into the armor after I swiveled the knees back to the front.

The damn suit is a thoroughbred and I'm trying to take a leisurely trot down a hallway!

A childhood memory flits across my mind of the day when I was twelve and my dad rented a power tiller. I hadn't expected that damn thing to drag me across the yard, but my dad thought it was a riot.

Reaching the elevator, I wait for Bryce to come work the controls while I lament not having built a true hand actuator instead of these tri-bladed claws. Like my lizard hybrid form, these claws are also kind of limiting. Pushing the elevator button isn't exactly easy.

Sometimes I forget that what might be utterly cool in a fight might be a pain in the ass when I'm not actually fighting. Better not mention this to anyone. The only one who wouldn't mock me is Andy, and he'd give me that kind of curious look that says he wouldn't have considered this idea in a thousand years . . . calling it stupid without actually calling it stupid. I don't need another reminder of that time when it was just me, Andy, and Bobby, I still had on the necklace that let me understand all languages, and I decided that because Assembly is a machine language that I could learn how to speak it..

It took a week for me to give up on that dream of walking up to Ultraweapon and telling his suit to turn off. I wouldn't be able to talk directly to technology. It would have been epic. Instead, I could watch porn from any country and not need the subtitles.

Bobby still tells that story, and I resist the urge to kill him—most of the time.

"Why didn't you press the button?" Bryce demands, strapping a holster with a plasma pistol to his side and then tapping something on his datapad.

"I push it with these, Captain Obvious, and I probably smash the controls. Seems like a really dumb time to take out the only elevator that leads to the lowest level when something stupid is going down."

That manages to shut him up, or the chirping from his datapad keeps his attention as we board and descend.

"You gonna share?" I ask, shifting in my suit uncomfortably. I might be nervous, or I might have shorted myself on the cooling system requirements. It's not like I can just start venting my excess plasma here, unless Mr. Leonardo wants that golden brown, deep-fried tan.

"Word on the street is that we're going to get hit by some supers and the *Federalis*."

"Wonder if it's reliable. Maybe it's a drill?" Figures there'd be someone connected enough to warn them and the Olympians wouldn't move unless they clear it with the government types. Yet another example of why unsanctioned super teams make perfect sense.

"Nah, I doubt it," he answers. "Praetorious wouldn't run one with so many hired hands around. You all just complicate things."

He has no idea how much I plan on complicating things!

We reach the bottom and the door opens. Instead of just the guard sitting at a desk, there are a pair of armed Type-A robots blocking the entrance to the high security lab. They shouldn't be much more than a speedbump on my way out of here with José, but I don't discount the problems they could cause.

"Pass him through, Yurkas. I need to get to my turret."

"I don't think this is a drill," the man with the shaved head states.

"Tell me about it, but if you want I'll trade places with you."

"No thanks. I'll ride it out down here. Watch your back out there, Leonardo."

I move toward the door while Bryce gets into the elevator. Apparently, there's a modicum of camaraderie amongst the foot soldiers of an archvillain. It cements the feeling that I'd have never fit in here. Sure, I am a nerd, a geek, but I'm not good in big groups. If some people are to be believed, I'm equally as bad in small groups.

Mangler's still down here, hunched over a fancy molecular analyzer, accompanied by White Rhino and a Mexican woman I don't recognize—one of the General's people, I have to assume. She's staring at a monitor and I see her cock her arm back and swing an open hand, in frustration, I guess.

"About time!" Rhino shouts.

If I had built five claws on each hand instead of just three, I'd give him the middle claw, but as it is, I simply can't spare a rat's ass for him. "What's going on outside?"

"Heroes and Mexican army," the woman answers and swings again. At that point I recognize her—2K Bitchslap! As powers go, the ability to deliver a stinging, open-handed smack across the face to anyone within two kilometers makes her hard to defend against, and terrifying to normal people without powers, but against anyone with a superpower, it is pretty lame and more of a distraction than anything else.

To be fair, who hasn't wished to bitch-slap from a distance? I still remember when that one president was getting sworn in and had to keep ducking while all the Secret Service scrambled around to find her. Considering I was watching from jail, that brightened my day. I promised I'd thank her for the laugh if I ever saw her. In a perfect world, I could hire her to harass that imposter who is pretending to be me.

"Please get the canister attached to his suit," Mangler orders Rhino in a calm voice that leaves no room for argument. "I must finish transferring the remaining data off the servers so we can depart. Mr. Harrell, the timetable for your field test has been abruptly moved up due to circumstances beyond our control."

I spare a glance at José. He is up and pacing nervously. Too bad I can't tell him how anxious I am right now.

Raising my arms, I let White Rhino attach the cylinder to the back of my suit. "How are you planning to get out of the base? Word is that there's only one way out and that's where the welcoming committee is."

"The less you know about our plans the better," Mangler answers. "I would concentrate on your own part in the battle, if I were you."

There's a grinding sound and the sprayer line pressurizes. I check the reading on the tiny digital gauge wired into my helmet. *Locked and loaded.* "What about him?" I gesture to José. "Bargaining chip?"

"And you care, why?" Rhino demands.

"I owe him for my transformation," I answer. "Wouldn't mind doing him in myself."

"Our heroic friend has made a valuable contribution to science, but I fear he is of no more use to us. He will be here when the equipment is destroyed. I hope this will satisfy your need for revenge. Regardless, it's time for you to depart."

That's what I figured! OK, play it off and head toward the door. I need a bit of space between me and White Rhino if I want to fight.

The suit is still hard to handle at low speeds and I stumble about fifteen feet away before I turn around and open my plasma vents and start lobbing plasma balls at Rhino, sending the woman and the withered husk of a scientist diving for cover.

Rhino and his outfit are on fire, but he screams and wastes no time pulling the rifle off his back. But I'm already accelerating toward him, firing more plasma bolts from the right arm and powering up the field around my left claw. Bitchslap's panicked blows start raining down on the suit, but they're useless.

The shield I installed eats most of Rhino's first shot, but I still feel the impact and stagger, lobbing a stream of plasma fire in his direction. It keeps Rhino pinned down behind one of the work tables. Even the thick skin of a Rhino is susceptible to plasma burns, and his screams of pain definitely aren't faked.

"I was worried that Praetorius would be here and I'd have to fight him," I say, bringing my powerclaw on the side room where they transformed and killed the clone. "Get ready to bounce, José!"

That's when one of my errant plasma discharges sets off an explosion in the room. The walls of the cell I just entered protect both me and the Gulf Coaster from the blast, but I suddenly start worrying about Mangler's toxins.

The inner door takes at least ten painfully slow seconds to hack through. "Keep your mouth covered and grab on," I shout.

José clearly has questions, but understands the seriousness of the situation. As soon as I feel him clamber onto my back, I take off toward the exit, hoping he won't end up a Mangler after all of this.

But it beats being dead.

I don't bother looking for the others. If there is any justice, Doctor Mangler will finally get a taste of his own medicine, and since the Rhino was involved in that ambush in Central America—screw him! The woman—well, that happens when you're a villain. The warbling alarms and fire suppression foam accompany our exit from the laboratory.

Bursting into the guard room, I see the guy named Yurkas fumbling with an emergency breathing hood and frantically pushing the call button. I yell for José to jump off because both of the Type-A robots grab me. More time ticks away as I slash away at the first robot. My Guardian pal slips by my wrestling match and sprints to the elevator.

A pair of lights on my HUD illuminates as I struggle with the pair of robots. Systems are being damaged, but all I worry about is whether my seal is intact or not.

After driving one of my whirling claws into the robot on my left and letting it wreak mechanical havoc throughout the bot's systems, I turn my attention to the other one. The arms on this unit aren't much stronger than my opponent's. However, I'm bolstered by the strength of my hybrid form, and that lets me turn the tables on it. I just slash away at it until it is no longer hindering me and push it away, willing the armor to get to the elevator.

There's an awkward pause as the three of us wait for the elevator. I can see Yurkas staring at his pistol belt, on the ground by his overturned chair. If it had just been José here, I'd lay even odds that the guard would try for it.

Further speculation is unnecessary because Yurkas collapses and starts having some type of seizure.

Shit! He's changing!

The door opens and thankfully, no one is in there. I'd half expected a damage control team or that the initial detonation would cause the elevator to stop running. Then again, everyone upstairs is preparing to repel the folks attacking the base. That should lower the quality of our opposition, but I'm not ready to do any kind of victory dance just yet.

"Let's go!"

"No! The guard!" José says, and grabs the man's legs. It takes a few more seconds before the twitching body is inside the doors and they are finally closing.

"Bad time to be doing the hero thing, Sixy!" I'd forgotten how heroes can abandon common sense at a moment's notice. It's like a disease—maybe herpes, considering the way it shows up at awkward times and makes even the simple things, like escaping, more complicated.

"What floor?"

Good question. All the fighting will be at the first floor and going out into the ground floor.

"Three," I say and point at the guy transforming right next to us. "We'll have to figure out what might be blocking our way out. Are you OK? You don't feel any...?"

"No! I seem to be fine, so far. Who are you, really?"

"Matt Harrell. I'm a U.S. government agent and I'm here to rescue you," I reply. The lie has worked pretty well up to this point.

He stares at me, and I start to wonder what's going through his head. "You called me 'Sixy' just a second ago. There's only one person who used to call me that."

Shit! Shit! And double shit!

"No, I didn't."

"I believe you did," he accuses. "This other person also was known for wearing armor."

I point a claw up at the elevator's ceiling and shoot the camera with a plasma ball. "Let's save it for later. OK, Sixy?"

Yurkas seems to be growing fur, and I wonder if he'll be predator or prey. If Mangler's theories about fear during exposure were true, it should be prey. I keep looking at my former team member to see if he shows any indication of changing. It'd be the peak of Mount Crapness if I rescued him only for him to change.

The door opens at level five instead of where we intended. There just happens to be a group of armed guards waiting there.

There's another awkward pause. This one includes weaponry.

A couple of them start to aim their guns.

I plow right into them and all hell breaks loose.

Chapter Twelve

When Four Heads Aren't Better Than One

Without a full head of steam, the armor struggles as I push my way through the guards. Omar designed this thing to be lightweight, and even though I have almost doubled the weight, it doesn't quite have the heft of any of my other suits, even Mana-CALes with the jetpack.

But I more than make up for the shortcomings of the VZ suit with my hybrid form's strength. I'm not facing any people with powers at the moment, so I start pushing my way through. I raise my left arm and activate the whirring claw blades while popping out plasma discharges.

"Who wants to die right now?" I shout. I'm sure I'm a terrifying sight. I'm also sure I'm kind of terrified currently, too.

Amazingly enough, they have the sense to fall over themselves trying to get away from me. I feel the rush of people being scared of me. It isn't something that I usually indulge in, but since it's a base full of villains and underlings, I don't really mind.

I'm slightly afraid of the turret unfolding from the wall. I bring the force-field-encased battle claw down on the center of it before the barrels finish lowering.

"Intruders on level five! Intruders on level five! Internal security, move to eliminate!"

José drags Yurkas's quivering form halfway out of the elevator and leaves him to keep it stuck on this floor. Next, he scoops up a couple of weapons from the ground and follows me. If there were more time, I'd tell him to swap out those white coveralls for some guard's clothing, but we need to lose these creeps and get to either the other elevator bank or a stairwell. If we make it to my workshop or some other defendable place, he can change there and we can barricade ourselves in until help arrives. I vent my plasma weapons at the cameras as I accelerate down the corridor. I stop and backpedal, returning to the man I freed.

"There's a stairwell left after the next junction and straight down the hall. We can try for that. I'll clear the way."

I sprint ahead and continue destroying the cameras on the path to the stairwell. A second turret extending out of the wall in front of the exit makes me reconsider my plan. We bolt back around the corner as it spins and starts firing much bigger bolts of plasma in my direction.

It's too far away for me to try and knock it out with my own weapons.

"In there," the Gulf Coaster says and points one of his pistols at a bathroom.

"Why?"

"No cameras. I've got enough strength to make a couple of clones. Four beats two, or we can use them for a distraction."

People underestimate José. I stopped doing that a long time ago. Like the Bugler, he works hard to be a hero. If there were more people like Bo and José, there'd probably be fewer resentful people like me around.

The bathroom is unisex with two normal stalls and one enlarged one for either handicapped access or a Mangler. Kudos to the designers for being up to code, but considering the woman in charge is a telekinetic paraplegic, it makes sense. One of the problems with remaining in my hybrid form for so long is that I did actually figure out how difficult it is to use the bathroom with reverse knee joints and a tiny tail that is just big enough to really get in the way when you're trying to take a dump.

Yeah, first world supervillain problems. I know.

Normally, it takes a couple of minutes for him to spawn a clone. Back in my Gulf Coast days, I'd seen him do it in about a minute.

I keep the door covered while he sets the two pistols on the sink and unzips the front of his coveralls.

As José's back begins to swell, I keep my eyes on the corridor and give him a modicum of privacy. A security team will be here soon, but they will be hampered by the attack going on outside.

"Warning! The emergency bulkheads are being sealed on level four and five."

That's going to slow me down, I think. The claws on this suit will be able to cut through, but it's going to take a whole bunch of time.

"Hurry up, José! They're going to try and keep us bottled up. We need to move!"

My ears catch the agonizing screams, letting me know something is most decidedly wrong with my Latino friend. Unlike most who have only ever seen videos uploaded to the internet about how José makes the six-pack, I have seen it in person, and it's never sounded excessively painful before. To my disbelief, José is lying on the white-tiled floor pounding his fist on the surface as a much-larger-than-normal fleshy cocoon continues to swell from his back. Something is definitely wrong!

There's a ripping sound as the cocoon is torn open. Stumbling out of the deflating mass is a fur-and-mucus-covered creature.

I can see confusion on the faces of both of them. Stepping closer, I see that the creature looks like a cross between José and a brown bear.

"José?" I ask. "Is that you?"

The hybrid nods and pulls the clone sac away from the human version of José, who is still staring in disbelief.

"I must have been exposed to the gas," the two of them say in unison.

"Sorry. I was prepared to just stay with you down there until they decided they were going to kill you. I know that might sound like a lame ass excuse, but it's the truth. Do you think all your clones are going to be Manglermals now?"

"It's possible. I can't really say," the human answers as the bear helps him stand. "We will just have to see what happens with the next one, but we need to get out of here first."

"Do you think your new buddy is strong enough to pick me up? I can use my power claws to break through to the level above us. It's probably easier than trying to cut through the safety doors. I don't think they'd be expecting that."

"Cut down instead," José says. "They only sealed this level in the one above us. They didn't seal the one below. The security guards will just assume my bear is another Mangler running about. He can clear a pathway to the stairs."

I have to admit that his plan is better than mine is, and probably more effective. Most of my ideas are the seat-of-the-pants kind, and like an old pair of jeans you pull out of the closet, they don't always fit like you think they should.

"Doing something is always better than doing nothing," I reply. "Better slide over into one of those stalls while I cut up the floor."

The bear version of José rips a stall door off with casual ease. He holds it behind him like a shield and puts his weight on the door. His voice is a ragged growl. "I will keep anyone from entering."

As I suspected, the floor is just concrete and natural stone. They do not provide the same challenge as the reinforced barricade. Still, I kick up a pretty large dust cloud and cause both of the Josés to break into a fit of coughing. With my reversed knee joints, I can get much lower to the ground than I thought. Even so, it takes some getting used to. The blaring alarms sort of cover the sounds of my cutting, and it takes roughly two minutes of the blades tearing away at the floor before I have a human-sized hole for us to go through.

"Hey Pooh Bear," I yell. "Pick me up and drop me down through the hole. It looks like another bathroom below us."

The human/bear hybrid rakes his claws along the tiles and digs a shallow trench in the floor. He jams the metal door into it and forces the other end underneath the handle, effectively sealing the room off.

"Perhaps I could get used to this," he says.

I am rather glad there are no cameras in here. Picture a bear picking up a lizard man in an armored speed suit in the middle of a dust-covered bathroom while a human watches. There's probably some fetish site that would pay good money to stream this.

My three-meter drop is surprisingly a rough one. I stagger when landing on the ground and bend the metal frames of the stalls. So you could say I didn't quite stick the landing. But as long as the point deduction doesn't result in one of us dying, I'll take it. Considering this is the first time I have used the suit, I'm actually shocked I'm not doing worse.

The Mangler follows me down after I stumble out of the twisted wreckage and holds his furry arms wide to catch the original José.

"Okay, head out into the hallway, turn right and try and get close enough to the turret to rip it out of the wall. Hopefully they'll mistake you for a plain old Mangler."

"Give me a ten-second head start and then come running!"

"Stay close to me and cover our backs with those pistols," I say to the human José.

"I can do that," he replies, coughing up some of the dust he'd gotten into his lungs one level up. He pauses and grins widely at me. "At some point, though, we have to have a discussion about who you really are, my old friend."

"Come on *compadre*, you know the old saying; unless you find the body, never assume someone is actually dead. It's the same with heroes, villains, and sarcastic assholes with a thing for powered armor. Much like the great Mark Twain, rumors of my death have been greatly exaggerated. Just do me a big favor and keep this between you and me."

He nods and slaps the shoulder of my armor. "If I must be truthful, old friend, what really gave it away is this shitty rescue."

"Any shitty rescue attempt you walk away from counts. Let's go!"

The entire facility shakes as we exit the sixth-floor bathroom, and I begin to wonder if all the fighting above is going to bring down the base on top of us.

A new series of alarms sound. A panic cry follows over the intercom system, stating, "There has been an explosion on level thirteen and we are detecting contaminants entering the ventilation system on level twelve! We can't shut down the system! Grab any breathing gear and hazmat suits you can before it's too fucking late!"

I take a quick, nervous glance at my suit pressure gauge, worried if it's going to hold now that Doctor Mangler's latest protocol is running around the ventilation system.

"Well, this rescue keeps getting better and better," José says with a bitter laugh. "Is the power plant on this level? Maybe you can activate the self-destruct while you're at it?"

"We're still not dead yet, so quit your damn complaining!"

Nothing impedes our progress to the stairwell. Once we get in there, it's my suit design that causes a fresh set of problems. The feet are slightly larger than the steps.

After a pair of falls getting to the next landing, the bear hoists me up while mentioning how now he has to rescue my sorry ass. Now the rescue part is becoming embarrassing.

On the fourth-floor landing we run across the Unfortunate Souls who must have been here to ambush us. Instead, three of the four have collapsed and are in the midst of their Manglermal transformations, while the fourth is probably dead.

"That's going to cut down on the good doctor's success ratio," I mutter.

Pooh Bear grabs a plasma rifle and rips off the trigger guard while his human counterpart stuffs both pistols into his coverall pockets and grabs a rifle for himself.

One upside to the situation is that we don't encounter anyone else until we make it to the door to the first level. We pop the door open, prepared for a fight, but instead it looks like one of those scenes out of a virus movie. Soldiers, technicians, and idiot middle managers are all shrieking on the floor as far as my eyes can see. There's a small part of me that feels an intense wave of guilt thinking about Gina, Dean, and even Bryce, but let's face it; these people deserve it more than the unsuspecting masses that would have ended up infected with this airborne version of the Manglermal protocol.

I spot a familiar red trench coat and see the owner on her knees staring at her paws with her one good eye. If I had to guess, Jeannie is now some kind of white tiger or maybe a snow leopard. It's tough to be sure. Still, considering how she treated me when she thought I was a Mangler, I can appreciate the irony of Blazing She-clops getting a special delivery of karma from the powers above or the venting gas below.

I guess she can be the One-Eyed She-Cat now, or maybe Blazing Feline?

"Keep moving toward the exit," the human José says.

I can see the ramp leading up to daylight and freedom. Unfortunately, I can also hear the sounds of a battle taking place.

"Right about now would be a good time to get them on the radio and let them know that we are coming out and not to blow us to pieces."

"Shit! I knew I forgot to install something in this armor!" I exclaim.

"You're kidding me, right? This is one of your stupid jokes again, isn't it? Sweet Mother Mary! You really are an idiot sometimes!"

In fairness, I didn't have all the time I needed to convert this armor over. Something was bound to get missed! "Look, grab on and I'll run us out of here. I'll try and find the first Olympian I lay eyes on and make sure they don't attack us. Keep your clone down here; he can do some good."

I accelerate up the ramp to find more than a few unaffected troops cowering behind barricades and firing their weapons toward the large number of vehicles surrounding the hangar.

Thinking quickly, I yell, "The gas is spreading up here! Unless you want to be turned into some kind of animal, we have to get out there and surrender! Hold your weapons in the air and follow us. Our only chance is to give them this prisoner!"

It takes only a few seconds for a couple of them to give in and the rest collapse like a bunch of Domino's. Self-preservation overrules a paycheck any day.

True, this is more self-serving on my part than looking out for the bubbas who work here. That's just me not wanting to be shot, and that is less likely when I'm leading a group of surrendering troops.

The midday sun leaves no shadows to hide in as my suit makes slow and jerky movements out of the hangar. The Mexican army has formed a semicircle roughly a quarter of a mile away from the hangar while all the supers are getting their freak on. I get a bad *Butch Cassidy and the Sundance Kid* flashback and hope this isn't my Bolivia.

It takes only a few seconds for me to spot Stacy in her Centurion armor. She's too far away, but she looks like a sandy, brown turd. I want to laugh when I see that she has a desert camouflage pattern for her color scheme. I realize that she likely had little input into this new look. Still, I will have to tease her about it, and that's all there is to it.

She and Ares are tag-teaming against Praetorius and look to be winning. *Figures, I finally get to see her in her suit, and I can't enjoy it.*

Just off to my right, I see an even more beautiful sight—it's the Megasuit laying a beatdown on a pair of Type-D warbots. *Still too dangerous for my current armor. There's Hestia and a mostly free path! Run! Run like hell!*

The goddess of home and hearth is using her psionic knives to stun various Manglermals. The four animated stone statues she controls are pulling the fallen fighters into a pile.

With José holding on, I sprint toward the person considered the least harmless of the Olympians and start dodging her energy knives.

"Hey! Take it easy. Good guy here with a Gulf Coast Guardian."

She pauses enough for José to wave at her.

"Good to see you, Six-Pack!"

"You as well!" he answers.

I stop and let José off me and gesture to the container of Mangler juice. "Unhook that cylinder. Considering how dangerous this shit is, I don't want it to explode." *Or if it does go off, I wouldn't want to be around it.*

It takes a minute for José to get it off me as I scan around the battlefield. Andy finished off the other Type D and has moved on to roughly a dozen Type-B rollers.

They're a little more my speed.

Breaking into a run, I head in that direction while firing some plasma balls at the swarm of gyroscopic balls rolling toward him. That should at least clue Andy in that I'm a friendly.

I hastily apply the brakes when all of Megas' weapons turn toward me. Boosting the external speaker to maximum, I shout, "It's me, Andydroid, Special Agent Matt Harrell. For the love of God, don't shoot!"

The gauss pistol swivels away from me, and seconds later another one of the Type Ds falls to the ground and does not attempt to rise. I briefly wonder if there's a service out there for robots who've fallen and can't get up.

"You do realize that the existence of an omnipotent being cannot be scientifically proven?"

"I've missed you too, buddy! Can you get on the horn and—"

My sentence is interrupted by an object smashing into me at ridiculous speed. I feel a sharp pain run up my left arm and then start to throb.

127

"Hello, Omar! Long time no see!" At least twenty punches strike the armor and I feel the dents start.

I shout, "I'm not Omar, idiot! Look at my legs. Do Omar's legs bend like this? I think you broke my damn arm!"

Hermes stops pummeling me. "Wait! What?"

I speak really slowly. "I . . . am . . . not . . . Omar! Didn't Athena brief you? If I was a villain, would I run over to the Megasuit just to say hello? I don't have a damn death wish."

She's still got a grip on my suit and her fist cocked. A series of conflicting emotions plays out on her face.

"Please unhand my colleague, Hermes. Otherwise, I will be forced to injure you." Andy's voice comes from behind.

She releases her grip on me. I'd like to think it is due to my expertly crafted argument, but who am I kidding? Mega is *my suit,* and I got scared when I was staring down its active weapons.

I take stock of my suit and notice the airtight seal is gone, somewhere between ten and fifteen punches ago.

Shit! This armor could be covered in Mangler juice! "Andy! Emergency decontamination."

"Explain the nature of the contagion."

"Their stock of Manglermal formula was released into the base's ventilation system! Better spray off Hermes as well. I doubt it could affect an Olympian, but it did turn She-Clops."

I know it is maybe thirty seconds while the plasma cannons rotate out and are replaced with fire hoses drawing from the lake at the base, but it feels much longer. *Is the magic protecting me? Will I change the moment I try to turn back into a human? It might be like José and be some kind of delayed reaction.*

As I fight the growing sense of panic, I use my right arm as a lever and force my suit upright. My other arm is dangling, and I deliberately glare at Keisha and channel my emotions into anger. She has the decency to look slightly embarrassed. The jets of water come out with enough force to make me brace the speed suit.

Dreading each second and waiting for any signs of a Mangler transformation to start, I turn and let Mega wash the back of my suit off. There's a bit of a flashback to my delousing in prison.

Quite frankly, I'm so done with today . . . this whole week while you're bullshittin'. I just want to crawl back through Mega's portal to our base, get my arm checked out, and take a week-long nap. That's not too much to ask, is it?

As Mega turns his water jets on Hermes, there is a sudden rumble that convinces me I've jinxed myself—again.

The ground explodes and a massive form leaps from the hole.

I hate it when I'm right!

After the pummeling the VZ suit took from the fastest person alive, it's a much rougher ride, but I put a little distance between me and the monster.

The thing almost defies description and is somewhere around twenty feet tall. It's furry in some places, scaled in others, and stands on eight thick legs. It has just as many arms, one human-ish and the rest a hodgepodge from the animal kingdom. The creature has a thick neck supporting four heads looking in all directions. The only one I can recognize is Igor Mangler's completely unchanged face, complete with a maniacal grin.

"Chimera!" It bellows from all four mouths.

Stacy delivers the first blow with the force blaster mounted on her suit. A tentacle lashes out, nowhere near the Centurion suit, but my girlfriend is knocked out of the sky.

Does that mean the fish head is 2KBitchslap? That means White Rhino must be there too. Not sure who the fourth one is.

A dozen or so Mexican soldiers and their armored personnel carrier turn their weapons on it, but they might as well be shooting spitballs. The Abomination calling itself Chimera partially disappears for a brief second only to rematerialize in the middle of the troops. Dr. Mangler's cheeks puff like a chipmunk before he releases a stream of liquid, as an arm that looks like it belongs on a praying mantis and a tentacle begin ripping the APC apart. The soldiers struck by the liquid immediately fall to the ground and began screaming. For a moment I fear he has venom sacs, but then I realize it's even worse; he is spitting Mangler juice.

Oh shit, this is not good! My little balls of plasma will probably only give this thing a skin rash.

A red blast of telekinetic energy interrupts my visit to my old stomping grounds of inadequacy, and I see Big Red has stepped in to try and wrangle the monster that I had a small hand in creating.

For a second it looks like Larry Hitt has Chimera in check, but then the creature does that disappearing act again and reappears about a hundred feet from where it was previously. I see a line of tilled Earth, and it takes me a few seconds to make the connection. The fourth person in that monster mashup must be Earthworm! The guy is another minor talent who could sort of teleport short distances through and along uninterrupted ground. To make matters worse, Chimera bitch-slaps Larry, who wasn't expecting any kind of attack from the creature.

I won't fault Larry for getting caught unprepared. He's still a rookie when it comes to being a renegade hero, and other than San Francisco, this is the biggest battle he's ever fought in. Before, when he was less than sane, he was just a tightly wound ball of rage. Now, Larry thinks before he acts—sometimes a little too much, and it gets him into trouble.

I accelerate in an attempt to get to Larry before that creature can attack him again.

Any worries that Chimera will pop on over and finish my buddy off are put to rest when the fish head and the insect head both pivot in my direction.

Four garbled voices shout in unison, "You! I'll kill you!"

Oh, that's not good, I think and peel away at a forty-five degree angle. Suit, don't fail me now!

VZ's leg actuators kick into high gear as I try to see how fast I can go from zero to sixty. As the built-in speedometer approaches eighty-eight miles per hour, I am sorely tempted to make a *Back to the Future,* joke but something beats me to the punch, sending me sprawling.

Chimera just bitch-slapped me!

My suit takes a tumble, but the gyros help me recover, and I stagger back to my feet, trying to make my escape from the monster who is teleporting closer and closer to me. Every hit sends a fresh stab of pain into my broken arm

Screw this! There's no way in hell I'll out run this thing. It's just going to toss me around like a rag doll, and I don't know how much more of a beating the suit can take. Why the hell didn't I put a jet pack on this thing?

With that in mind, I swerve and change directions. My new plan is to lead it back to where everyone who has guns can shoot the damn thing or at least slow it down to where I can get out of its line of sight. My legs churn away, spitting dirt in my wake, and I throw as much plasma behind me as the one usable arm I have can jettison. It's little more than a fireworks show, but I'm not about to give up now.

I try switching back and forth, but it's no use. The next bitch-slap at least send me closer to the people who can fight Mangler and company.

Megasuit moves to cover me. Plasma cannon fire forces the abomination to do the teleport thing again.

"Use the railgun!" I shout. "Finish him!"

"You know very well why I will not do that," Andy says.

Ironic, isn't it. The most lethal weapon on the planet is in the hands of an android programmed not to kill. Does anyone besides me see a problem with that? Yeah, I thought so.

"Kill you!" Someone obviously doesn't have the same problem my friend does.

Andy fires again, forcing my would-be murderer to dodge. "You have a singular ability to make people want to kill you."

"Less clever observations and more weapons fire. If you won't kill it, could you at least severely injure it?"

"That also would not be permissible."

I take a moment to compose my reply—mostly because I am being bitch-slapped again. "Then get Wendy or Larry! Get it off the ground! It won't be able to teleport."

Over VZ's limited interface protesting this continued treatment, I try to rise, or at least cower behind the Megasuit. The alarm is more of an angry chirp than the warbling klaxon I always use in my suits for a master alarm. I actually like it better. Maybe it's time for a change.

Great! I probably have a concussion, if I'm wasting time thinking about crap like that.

The tentacle snaps back and I take another hit. At least I'm already on the ground and don't have far to fall. The suit cuts off in mid chirp. I'm strong enough to move in it by myself, but I'm obviously not going to get far.

"Andy," I shout. It comes out slurred. "Get me out of here!"

Megasuit hoists me like a sack of potatoes, and I hear the roar of the thrusters since my head is dangling over his shoulders. It's oddly soothing, even though we both take several more slaps. Mega absorbs most of the sting, but I get my bell rung two or maybe three times.

I've had a rough few days. The rest of them can clean up without me. Yeah, a nice long nap would be good right about . . .

Chapter Thirteen

The Unsightly Aftermath

The first thing I hear is the slightly monotonous drone of medical equipment as my consciousness finishes a cold boot. I still feel a little fuzzy. If I really were like Andy, I'd consider running a defrag or some kind of kernel checker on my mind.

Since I can't, I go over what I can remember, getting tentacle-slapped around in the middle of Northern Mexico like one of those perps on a bad cop show. Definitely not going into my victory scrapbook.

I force one of my eyes open. There's a tabby cat's face staring at me. I jump in surprise, but don't get too far because I seem to be restrained.

Seconds pass as I stave off the shock and momentary panic. I'm not in a hospital, but in James and Flora's first floor master bedroom at the fake bed and breakfast above the Alabama base. It doubles as our clinic. Down in the base, we have a gurney and some decent first aid supplies, but not enough room for anything much more than that. I must have already been there, done that, gotten the T-shirt, and been moved to our more comfortable accommodations.

Flora, an expression of Andy trying to get in touch with his female self, has decorated the room. She has an eye for abstract art, vases, those little angel figurines, and a holographic cat. Wendy didn't want Flora to get a real one. Andy rebelled and built Flora a virtual pet.

It's night out, but that doesn't really tell me much. It's a good guess that I am never going out in the field again, and I mean ever. Seriously, I might never leave the base again.

The door is thrown open and instead of the cosmetically enhanced Type-A robots, I'm treated to Bobby Walton. Instead of a stethoscope and a medical chart, he has a beer and a bag of chips.

And they say medical care is on the decline!

"Hey there, Lizardboy! 'Bout damn time you finally wake up. Brings back memories of how badly you used to get your ass kicked all the time! Whatsamatter? Did you run into the Biloxi Bugler again and get another whuppin?"

Bobby lacks a bedside manner or any manners in general. I may have to revisit my statements from a few seconds ago.

I let the Bugler comment slide. I have considerably more respect for Bo Carr than I did back in the day. Bobby is just yanking my chain. It's his way of showing he cares.

I think I need better friends.

"How long was I out?" I groan, noticing that I'm still in my hybrid form. My lisping voice is further butchered by a dry, rasping cough.

"Been about ten hours, give or take. You were pretty jacked up."

The arm I had been worried that Hermes broke is in a cast and I have a leg elevated in traction. Ugly bruises cover it, but I can't feel it. My reversed knee joint has a circular pain suppressor wrapped around it. It's like a white noise generator for pain. Promethia bought out the company that planned on making these as inexpensive as possible and decided to pad their bottom line instead.

When they make something to cancel out bitter feelings, I'll ask Wendy to buy one for me. Either way, I seem to be in no immediate danger.

"How's my suit?"

"Mega? Or that piece of shit you came in with?"

"Both, but I'm sure Andy wouldn't let anything happen to Mega, so the VZ suit."

"I had to pop you out of it after Andy flew you away. It wouldn't fit up the chute with you in it, and I didn't exactly know where all them releases and whatnot were. And, you have to understand, it wasn't exactly in great shape to begin with. Well, you know—"

Cutting him off, I say, "So, what you're saying is that it's pretty jacked up, too."

He gives me an unapologetic shrug. "Yeah, sorry 'bout that. But you should be grateful, I coulda stuck around and hit on Hermes. Word on the street is that she wants to take a ride on the Highwayman!"

"No biggie," I reassure him, cringing inside at the thought of the Olympian and Bobby together. "I'd planned on tearing it down anyway and maybe wiring it up for Andy to use with us out in the field. As for Hermes, make sure you keep the motorcycle helmet on."

Bobby visibly relaxes. *He actually is worried that I'm pissed about the armor.*

"You could have taken off the belt and treated me like a human. Did Andy decide I was too injured to take a try at it?"

There's a long pause while Bobby frowns. "We did. Just a few minutes after we brought you through. Andy even put it in a box with a force field on it to see if it would break the flow of the magic or some such shit. It's in your room down in the base."

I think I'm allowed to panic at that. It's a perfectly reasonable reaction to an unreasonable situation.

"Is it just the magic, or did I get exposed to the Mangler juice?"

"Cal!"

"Shit! Shit! Shit! Come on, man! Spit it out, Bobby!"

"Do you seriously think I know the answer to that? C'mon, Cal! You'll have to wait until Andy is free. He's got some ideas about what's going on."

He's right. The mere fact that I'm asking Bobby for a medical opinion just shows how desperate I am. Andy can multitask better than any living being, but the android's program restricts how many instances he can have at any given time.

I take a few minutes to stop hyperventilating. Now I can add a slight sense of lightheadedness to my list of current medical issues.

Focus.

Don't panic!

Focus.

Seriously, don't panic!

Focus!

"Screw it!" I shout. The logical portion of my mind says that maintaining the hybrid spell for consecutive several days has probably led to where I'm magically saturated, and staying away from magic for the near future will allow it to drain off and nullify the spell. Maybe I could get Bobby to open a window and I could shoot a mage bolt or two and try and bleed off some of the excess. Then again, maybe I could just shoot one at Bobby and get a little satisfaction out of it at the same time.

Instead of giving in, I wave my free clawed hand at Flora's jewelry box and levitate it to start getting rid of the excess I've built up.

Of course there's a minute chance that I have reached an oversaturated condition. It's kind of like the expression "Don't make that face or it might get stuck like that." I'm not too worried about that. Everyone who Tyrannosorcerer Rex changed reverted back when I offed his cold-blooded ass. Of course, he was holding the spell over several hundred people. I also ran around a base where a cloud of airborne mutation gas was released and who knows whether any got on me or not. The odds aren't really in my favor, but that's pretty much the story of my life.

At the very least, I hope that I will change back when I die. Then again, that would negate the chance of my body ending up in some kind of sideshow attraction.

I find it's best to face these situations with humor. It helps with the panic.

• • •

"You still haven't changed back." Wendy states the obvious, entering the room. Her arm is in a sling because of the break in her collar bone. "I wanted to bring Gabby by, but am holding off until you do."

"It's been almost two days," I hiss. "This is starting to get old. It shouldn't be a problem if you want to bring her to see me. I tried three times spending what little magic I have until I pass out. All that got me was a couple of good naps. Andy sent Flora and James in twice to give me a decontamination scrub down. See how shiny my scales are?"

She smiles, and I know she's got a zinger prepared and is just waiting to use it. "Maybe you need a kiss from a princess to break your evil spell?"

"You volunteering?"

"I ain't no damn princess! Hell, between you and me, you're the one who is usually the damsel in distress."

"Way to kick a hybrid when he's down," I retort. "So, other than taking a couple of cheap shots at me, and demonstrating your obvious bigotry against semi-humans, what are you doing here?"

"Some things have come up that you need to be in the loop on."

I really don't like the way that sounds. I set down the laptop that's playing the images of the battle and the aftermath. I can't be sure why, but I am somewhat interested in what happened to Bryce and Dean. Gina, I spotted. Or at least, I saw a sort of attractive female bunny hybrid with a blue and purple tinge to the fur on her head in a tattered set of scrubs. Who knows where she goes from there? I feel somewhat bad for her, but in the end she is a nice sort of person who works for a really bad person. She also made the mistake of befriending a guy who lies to everyone, including himself.

Hermes found her cousin, now a cheetah-themed Mangler, still unconscious in the recovery unit. It appears that he's going to live and be pissed that someone stole his armor.

"Let's just wait, shall we? I watched a couple of Mexican soldiers come up to shake José's hand and give him a pat on the back," she says.

"Let me guess, two new Manglermals?"

"You're not as dumb as you look . . . at least right now."

My free hand is still missing two fingers, but I give her the middle claw anyway. It's the thought that counts. Then I have to get serious for a change. "Is Larry okay?"

Wendy pauses and looks for the right words. "He's getting there. I assured him that I was going to take the four-headed monster out, if he hadn't. Why else did I updraft it probably a thousand feet in the air? I didn't know about Bitchslap, and Larry reacted to me getting hurt. I don't consider what he did an issue, but he is afraid of his powers at the moment and closing himself off."

I shake my head at her. Wendy is somewhat understating the situation. Larry ripped Doc Mangler and his three buddies in half. Or is that halves? Quarters? Either way, chunks of the creature rained down on the battlefield and pretty much put a halt to all the fighting.

"I was hoping Andy would use the railgun or just hand me the damn thing and let me take the shot. I wasn't too keen on you having to be the one, and I sure as shit never wanted any more blood on Larry's hands. That's what you have me and Bobby for. We're the heavies. We're the ones that wash death away with a case of beer."

"We don't always get what we want," the petite brunette states. "I am thinking of sending him up to talk with you. Bobby tried having words with him, but I think this is more up your alley."

She must be worried. She hasn't cussed very much!

"Have you spoken with Stacy at all? Is she coming?"

"She's stuck at the site of the battle. Her armor makes her one of the few that can safely go into the quarantine area without any fear of exposure. I let her know what's going on with you and asked her to stay away for a few days. I didn't think you'd want her to see you like this. I can get with Andy and have him rig something up so you can talk with her."

That is actually very considerate of Wendy. Shit! She must be on the verge of freaking out over her team with me injured, and what's going on with Larry. "No. Tell her I don't mind if she stops by. Actually, I think you should have her talk with Larry."

"Her? Really?"

"Yeah. Stacy has been at the game as long as you have. She knows the deal, and understands how bad things can go. Larry knows what I'm capable of, and would expect me to tell him to walk it off or some such shit. He's got a kid sister thing going on with you. Hell, you could go on a homicidal rage in a daycare and Larry wouldn't think any less of you, but Stacy isn't really part of our team. If an Olympian tells him that he did the right—well, that he did what was necessary—it'll mean something more. I think she can get through to him."

The Overlord had compared Larry to The Cowardly Lion from The Wizard of Oz. *He wasn't certain Larry had the stomach for some of the darker things that come with being a hero. Larry will probably find himself in this position again if old Jerimiah has his way.*

"I really hate it when you start making sense. Anytime you do, I feel like there should be some emergency right behind you."

"I'm fresh out of emergencies at the moment. Check back in a few days, I should have something by then."

"Funny," she replies in a tone that conveys how little she thinks of my joke. "We're in a bind here. I'll be honest, I'm going to send Flora back in here to decontaminate you one more time. I need you back in control of the Megasuit. Andy's working on reconfiguring a chair you can sit in in this form and keep that leg up."

"Sounds serious. What's wrong?"

"Wrong? Well, let me tell you what's fucking wrong! José says Mangler boasted that they'd already sent enough out of the previous formulas to make five bombs."

"Five? He didn't sound like he was nearly that far along!"

"Oh, he was. He just wanted to get as close to one hundred percent and was after a version that would work on supers. Mangler didn't like the idea of anyone being immune to his creation."

"There's still that one canister. They wanted me to go spray Spiritstaff and K-Otica. Let me guess. Either the government of Mexico or America grabbed it so they could study it for a potential cure, but really just wants to perfect the process."

"I took it," she answers, positively stunning me.

"Holy shit! No way!"

"After the thing with those little invulnerability patches, I'm not ready to trust any government with that shit. The Mexicans are lining up volunteers to go in to the quarantine zone to 'help salvage.' What they're really doing is making a Mangler special ops regiment and collecting as much of Mangler's formula as they can. It seems to be losing potency from what José passed on to me."

I can see that my dreams of stealing all the shit out of that base or just taking it over are going up in flames. So much stuff, all contaminated and in someone else's hands. *What a goddamn waste!*

She continues, "The formula even un-Mangled one guy. Turned him from a minotaur back into a regular guy."

"Babe?"

"Call me that again," she threatens. "See what happens."

"No, Babe the Blue Ox. Was it that guy?"

"Oh, yeah. I think so. Sorry," she says, clearly a bit out of sync. "José wants to come by as well. He cornered me and let me know he was on to you. Nice job keeping that a secret."

"I try."

"How about trying a little harder next time, Cal?"

"Sure thing, boss!" I shout back with false cheer. "I should have known he'd recognize me transformed into a lizard, not being dead, and replaced by an imposter. What was I thinking?"

"You make it real easy to fucking hate you. You know that?"

"You're forgetting who came up with this great idea. How is the Six-Pack, anyway?"

"His clones come out and immediately change into Manglers. He appears to be as human as they come, but every clone so far has been a different kind of Mangler."

"Is he OK with that?" I ask. "You could call it an upgrade, but it is kind of a shitty one."

"Charles said that José is dealing with it as expected. He might send one of his clones out to stay with us. It would make coordination easier between our teams since Paper Tiger can't be in two places at once. José is even considering a name change."

"To what? With the right combination, he could call himself *The Five Deadly Venoms*. I always loved that movie. Beastmaster? Zookeeper?"

"*Casa de Fieras* or Menagerie in English," she answers. "Although Beastmaster in Spanish might sound better . . . *El Maestro de Bestia?*"

I shrug and wrap my claws around a plastic cup of water. Using a straw is a little odd when your head is partially reptilian and doubly so when you're drinking a beer. Who does that? Right now, I guess I do. "Sounds long-winded to me. I would stick with Six-Pack or maybe start calling himself Wild Pack."

"If my mom was managing him, she would probably recommend Wild Pack. It's close enough to his old name to keep the branding, but new enough that he could probably have his agent renegotiate licensing fees."

I had forgotten the whole business aspect of things. Being a criminal previously, I didn't have any rights with the toy companies until I joined the Gulf Coasters. The Mechanical—yeah, even they didn't bother getting the name right—action figure had originally been included in the limited run Biloxi Bugler Bank heist playset. The toy company reissued it after I was no longer in the picture and threw in a couple of generic thugs action figures. Suddenly it became a hero "team up" set.

Bobby bought me an unopened original version as a gag gift just before I "died" off in California. It is actually a pretty valuable collectible now.

When I switched sides, the PR group handling the Guardians negotiated the standard licensing deal for my MK III suit and the name correction. Last I heard, the imposter is sailing on that revenue stream.

"So what's on the agenda, boss lady? I know you can't get enough of me and all that, and we obviously have to track down the Mangler bombs, but I am guessing there's more."

She collects her thoughts for a moment. "We need to start putting together a plan to deal with that fucking imposter of yours."

It's funny how a near-death situation can make me forget that there is someone else out there pretending to be me and reaping the rewards of my hard work. It's yet another example of first-world superhuman problems.

"What's he done now? More interviews badmouthing heroes? I actually kind of enjoy those. Whoever it is, he is a much better public speaker than I ever will be."

She turns on the television and thumbs through the menu for a recorded segment on the Superhuman News Network.

I see a very human version of me, standing at a podium and not looking at all uncomfortable in a business suit. Anyone who really knows me would realize that I'm more at home in a powersuit than one of those damn things!

Beside my doppelganger is my co-novelist, Megan, a woman I recognize as a big-time attorney, and two others. One is a man in a purple and reddish suit with a matching fedora. The other is a smallish red-headed college-aged female dressed like she's headed to her first interview.

The guy is The Fabulous Gay Mage, and I only recognize the co-ed because Bobby fought her a few weeks ago—Treehugger. The Mage is a solid B-level magician and obviously a threat to my Megasuit with his spells. Treehugger is strong and fairly mobile because she can teleport into trees and turn them into her new body. I rate her as a high C or maybe on the low side of the B level.

He's bought himself a pair of bodyguards. That's not a good sign. He probably pays them with my money!

Onscreen, my mouth begins moving. "After the events in Mexico, I have to express my concern over my daughter's safety. Allow me to be perfectly clear—Wendy is and always will be a great hero. Right now, she's in a spot of trouble with our government. I've been there and done that, so I'm not the one to throw stones when I'm living in a glass house. Still, it isn't about Wendy, it's about my little girl. What kind of life can she be living on the run? She should be playing, making friends, and doing all the things that kids her age are supposed to be doing, not hidden in some dark corner of a secret hideout. I've been patient, but I'm a father who has never even held his daughter. I don't think I can wait much longer knowing she's out there and possibly in danger."

There are a few seconds of silence before the bastard moves on. "To that end, I've filed a request with the court to terminate Wendy's rights as a parent and asked the FBI to classify Gabby as being abducted."

Even though the imposter hadn't finished, a flurry of questions interrupted him. I see the faintest hint of a crack in that mask the copy wears. He tries not to get overwhelmed before Megan pushes him aside.

"What Calvin is saying is that while he understands and appreciates all the contributions that Wendy LaGuardia has made, the child Calvin helped her conceive needs to be in a stable environment. Mr. Stringel has the money to hire bodyguards and support the baby. Some people believe that this is a conspiracy that the government would use his daughter as leverage over WhirlWendy. Cal and his team have been in contact with the Superhuman Activities committee and have been assured by multiple congressmen on that committee that this would not be the case. As my client is somewhat famous, any action against his baby would draw the kind of negative response that every government official runs and hides from.

"Furthermore, I think it's obvious which way the vaunted superhumans she associates with are going to side. Despite being a fugitive and having several warrants out for her arrest, none of the Olympians or her fellow Guardians made any attempt to detain her in Mexico. I would certainly hope that the leaders of those groups have to justify their actions, or should I say inactions, to the government. They're most assuredly thumbing their nose at the people who fund their teams and permit their teams to have a legitimate existence. Maybe the truth is that they are looking at Wendy and her rogue team as an example of where they want to take their teams."

I have to hand it to Ms. Bostic. She really dislikes supers. I'd say that she has an ax to grind, but she's ground it for so long that all she has left is a wooden handle.

Wendy cuts off the video. "There's more, of course. Not only is he filing for custody of Gabby *in absentia* and has made an official request asking the FBI to bring federal kidnapping charges against me, but he's also filed a civil case against my mom for aiding after the fact, because she met us in Cuba."

"Well, that is a little more serious than being an asshole on TV. It's definitely not something I intend to let slide. Do you want to go with the reveal angle? I liked it better when people thought I was dead, but now that I'm technically alive again, it's a new story. The only problem that I can see is that we'd have to find a new base. Even with the bit of misdirection in my book about the location of this place, our enemies would definitely figure out a way to find us here. We'd need time to find a new place and more time to move everything there. I could see us operating off a container ship in international waters."

Wendy exhales, blowing her bangs away from her eyes. "I don't think we can afford to be down anytime soon while Devious is out there plotting. At this point I would be willing to just turn a blind eye and let you do as you please to the fucking poser. Go make yourself dead again if you want."

"I can't believe that I'm the voice of reason here. You can't; he dies now at my hands, and they try to frame it so you ordered his death."

I leave out the fact that she essentially just gave me the green light. That would make an already awkward conversation worse.

"Pretty much. Holy shit, this is frustrating! I am used to just having Mom send out the lawyers to deal with this kind of crap."

"You know she can still do that."

"True, but it's not going to be nearly as effective with me in hiding. You specialize in out-of-the-box thinking. What have you got for this?"

Wendy can't confront the fake me. I can't do it in Mega, either. What about VZ? I could maybe use that. No. We might need special agent Matt Harrell again, and that fake ID is already associated with us. What about borrowing one of José's Manglers, since he knows the truth? *Oh, I think I'm missing the obvious here.*

"Bobby is still technically a criminal. Plus, I wasn't very generous to him in my book, now was I? He reminds me of it all the time. I could see him going out west to rough my imposter up a little—or a lot—and just call it a personal grudge."

My leader scowls, and I'm not sure whether it's because we're talking about killing someone or because she would have to trust Bobby to do the deed.

"If it was just the clone or shapeshifter or whatever the hell he is, I think Bobby would be a good option. However, your counterpart has been citing death threats against him as a reason to acquire those two bodyguards we saw. He's negotiating for a third, if what SNN is reporting is true."

"I'm a little wary of fighting a decent magic user. I need to avoid FGM like the plague. I'm magiphobic, not homophobic. Bobby handled the girl well enough when the two of them tussled up by DC."

"But I don't like Bobby's odds against the two of them, or more if your imposter is really a shape changer."

"What if we had him spend some cash and put a Revenge Crew together to go after me?"

"No. No. Fuck, no! I can't believe we're even considering it!"

"Why not? I think it is a good idea. It'll work, too."

"I'm not going to hire a bunch of Supervillains to kill someone. That's just . . . that's just . . . that's just all kinds of . . . No! Forget I even told you about this!"

I drag my claws along the rail of my hospital bed. "He's not exactly just your problem," I say. "I called dibs on him from the get-go. You told me to wait until we rescue José before going after the fake. José is back—a little worse for wear, but we have him. Right now, legal shit can take a back seat to finding Devious and those Mangler bombs. Hey! You said you grabbed that one canister of Mangler's improved formula I was carrying. We've seen it can work on some super humans, maybe we should introduce the imposter to it and see how long before he cracks."

Wendy is speechless, and I've rarely seen her in that state. "I can't say I like that idea any better than killing him, but I'm not entirely against it. The hero community in general would cheer if you somehow got Bostic as well."

"I always thought she was cool, but I can see why others don't have my enlightened—ahhhh shit!"

My cry of pain interrupts my witty reply. It feels like someone has taken a blowtorch to the nerves surrounding my injuries.

"Cal, are you OK?"

Even Wendy can unleash a stupid question every now and then. The only answer I can give her is another painful scream. With blurry vision, I stare at my arm in the cast. The claws are shrinking and starting to change color. As long as I have a reason for it, I can deal—at least for the most part. I grit my teeth, even as the fangs round off and I hear a nasty pop from my jaw that would make any dental hygienist cringe.

The cast splits open as my arm elongates and straightens. The light green gives way to my normal pinkish hue. It's just as painful as breaking it the first time.

When's this shit going to end? Seriously!

I feel my body seize up like an engine with no oil and I fall out of the hospital bed. I hit the floor, leading with my chin, performing an Olympic-level face plant. After five seconds there's a release, like a rubber band snapping.

"Ugh!" I note there is no hiss or lisp to my voice. My body feels as if I spent too long in a sauna, but otherwise I'm not in the same level of pain. I am exhausted, but no longer cold. The oversized shorts, with the big slit in the back for my tail, are now pooled around my ankles.

The arm feels much better. The transformation must've healed it. I send a quick glance in the direction of my bruised leg. All the bruises are gone, too!

"Guess that's why I didn't turn back. My body needed to heal first," I say, trying to get used to what I sound like again. "How do I look?"

"As ugly as ever and you're naked," Wendy answers. "Mind covering up? It's not supposed to be a full moon tonight."

"Nothing you haven't seen before," I reply and make sure "Little Winky" is now "Regular Winky." I push up and climb to my feet, swaying uncertainly. Deciding to play it safe, I fall back onto the hospital bed and crawl in as best as I can.

"Magical healing," I say pulling a sheet back over my naked form. "That's a new and rather painful option."

She walks closer and picks up the things I knocked over during my transformation. "You probably slowed things down by draining your magic."

"Nice to know your hindsight is a perfect twenty-twenty, Ms. LaGuardia."

"Hold still, you big baby. Let me reattach your blood pressure cuff. We probably need to run some tests on how fast you can heal before I think about sending you out again."

I put my figurative foot down. It happens to be human again. "Who says I'm ever going back out again? I'm gonna have to say no."

Wendy shakes her head at me. "You don't always get what you want, Cal. Trust me on that one."

Knowing she's right, but still wanting to stand my ground, I roll my eyes like a teenager and say, "Whatever."

"Well, now that you're back to normal and haven't turned into a Mangler, I think I'll go get your daughter. Well, after one more Flora and James scrub down. Oh, Andy! Send in the nurses."

Great! Animatronic Silkwood. Well, at least my skin will be nice and soft when Gabby gets here. The shit I put up with!

Chapter Fourteen

The Last Moment Just Before the Fall

"So does this magical healing thing mean you want to get a little freakier?"

I laugh at Stacy as she gathers me into a crushing hug. Bobby always gives me shit that with her strength, the Olympian has to be gentle with me.

"Funny. Say what you want, but I'm the one that's sleeping with you. You're stuck slumming with me. But, the magic only seems to work going from lizard to human. So, unless you're talking about a whole new level of freaky, I think you need to dial it back some. It's good to see you, even if you didn't bring your suit with you this time."

"No, I want you all to myself," she says. "We can play 'what gadget Cal wants to put into my armor' next time."

Giving her the pouty face, I say, "Next time, I guess. Do you want to go down and see everyone first or take a walk with me?"

"Let's walk."

I fall in beside her and ask a question, "Did the telepaths get in to Praetorius's mind? The UN must be scared since they voted in favor of it as soon as they found out Devious has more Mangler bombs."

"They were making some progress, but Praetorius killed himself. He snapped his own neck. That hasn't been released to the public yet."

"Who am I going to tell?" I say after a dry chuckle. "Do you think he did it himself, or did Devious set some kind of mental trigger?"

"No one is certain. He bit his tongue intentionally to draw blood. Before he died, he wrote 'My Life Ends and Her Reign Begins' in his blood on the wall."

"Cryptic and concerning at the same time."

"Yeah, I wanted to get away before she makes her move, because I'm not certain how much time we have. Do you mind if we change the subject?"

"Anything you want," I say and raise my eyebrows in a suggestive manner.

"Is that an offer or a challenge?" Stacy answers. Her smile appears a little forced and she looks weary, like she's seen too much lately.

I know what I have to do—distract her and take her mind off things. Wendy tells me my superpower is being able to distract people. Technically, she said it was being a world class pain in the ass, but I like to think she means that in a good way.

"Well, anything except swimming. It's a little too cold to take a dip in the pond, at least for me."

Late fall and early winter in Alabama isn't so bad. What can I say? I like to be warm. The love goddess isn't bothered by heat or cold. She regularly goes skiing in a bikini, and I've seen her walk across a bed of hot coals and treat it like it was just warm beach sand.

We kiss out by the pond and I breathe in her smell. "I've missed you. It's been too damn long. You live for several millennia. I still say that you should get them to advance you a few years of vacation time and we forget about all this stupidity and go hang out in the tropics."

How does her retirement plan work? Does she have to work until she's three thousand and they pay her for the next thousand years? I'll save that for when I need an odd question to keep her on her toes.

"I wish it was that simple," she says, with a hint of sadness in her voice. "There's too much going on in the world right now. Robin told me that the Esper team that advises the president lost one of their members to a mental breakdown, and the other two are predicting doom and gloom. The last time they got this worked up was right before the whole thing with the bugs."

"I don't put much stock in soothsayers," I answer and squeeze her hand. "They're worse than those people who try to tell you what the weather will be tomorrow. What is the damn difference between partly cloudy and mostly sunny anyway? Maybe I'll try my hands at old Viking runic magic and 'throw the bones around'."

Her smile fades and I see her frown. "Seriously though, Cal, I'm worried. You told me that you had trouble turning back."

"My guess is that my body needed to be strong enough to heal."

"That's just your best guess, Cal. You don't really know for certain."

"Well, yeah. But it's the best working theory I have right now, and Wendy agrees."

She shakes her head a couple of times and I can see the worry. "Theories can be wrong. You're in untested waters here. You're not playing with regular human magic. That alone would be bad enough, and I can't tell you the number of times heroes have had to deal with people who've had a taste and wanted much, much more. But you're dealing with magic created by non-humans—something that predates the Olympians and maybe even the Titans. You could do some serious harm to yourself."

"I'll be careful," I say. "But I need every advantage I can get."

"You don't," Stacy replies. "You've got Megasuit and the magic to fall back on. How much more do you really need? I get it. You're always tinkering and trying to improve. It's one of your best traits and it can be one of your worst at the same time."

For the first time since she came back into my life, I'm starting to feel a little irritated with my girlfriend. Of course, being an empath, she's probably caught wind of it already.

"Sorry," she says, raising the hand that I'm not holding in a gesture of peace. "I'm not back in your arms for five minutes and I'm lecturing you. You're important to me, Cal. And I know you pretty well now. You won't be more careful, but I am asking you to be less reckless."

"It's annoying how you can just turn an argument around before it gets any traction."

She laughs and shakes her shoulder-length hair. "Make love, not war is my motto. Plus, I didn't come here to fight with you. Why don't we borrow one of the beds in the bed and breakfast for a couple of hours before I go have my first sit-down with Larry and see if I can help him out of this funk? I think I need someone to get me out of my funk first. Are you up for it?"

"Ready, willing, and able. What will I do while my beautiful girlfriend is counselling my friend?"

"Well, I might have a crate of drone components in the back of the van. You can play with those while I work with Larry."

"You brought me a gift? What? Did you just waltz up to the Department of Defense and tell them that you need a drone and if you could get it for me this weekend that'd be great?"

She ignores my movie pun. "Actually, I went to Bo and told him that I was looking to make my own version of your floater. He didn't even blink before giving me a base unit."

I nod. Bo and I joked about my becoming The Drone Master when I couldn't put a working suit together during my Gulf Coast days. Though he'll never quite shed the Biloxi Bugler name, Mr. Carr seems to be settling into the role quite well.

"What do you want in it?"

"Surprise me," she answers, and adds a flirtatious smile as we reach the door to the fake bed and breakfast. "I want to see what you can come up with, but I'm guessing you probably need some encouragement."

"I believe I would like to be encouraged. It helps me work."

As we enter the atrium, she uses her strength and hoists me over her shoulder like I'm a sack of potatoes. Surprisingly, I'm OK as a conquest, as long as she doesn't do some kind of "caveman drag me by my hair" thing, I'm good with it.

Well, let's be honest. Even if she did want to do that, I'd probably still be good with it. Don't judge me!

• • •

As my girlfriend tries to get to the bottom of Larry's issues, I'm working on the four-rotor hover drone she's provided.

So many choices!

I need to do something impressive. We came close to what was going to be a huge argument. She does have a point—when will it be enough for me?

I'm pretty sure the answer is never, but a little megalomania never hurts, right?

"Hmmn," I say out loud. "I can fit about twenty-five pounds of payload on here, and since I can run the power through a small crystal shard, I can get more bang for the buck. If I just wire the drone with shield emitters and have the shield generator here in the base, I could still have the space for . . . "

I drift off for a second as several variations of this new drone flash in my mind. It quickly escalates to where I imagine it as a floating railgun platform.

The drone to end all drones! Because that would be totally insane! I should totally do that!

Sadly, I don't have room down here for a second magnetic cannon and the power it would require; the struggles of a former D-List Supervillain are all too real. Plus, I'm not about to give up mine. Stacy will just have to settle for a plasma cannon, unless . . .

Hey, what about . . .

Oh yeah. That could . . .

No one would see that coming!

Unfortunately, I'm dragged out of my moment of inspiration by the sound of my voice on the television that I'd been running for background noise. Hearing the imposter moves it up into the foreground and pushes aside my plans for Stacy's Totally Awesome Drone (or STAD) for the moment while I see what anti-super-powered rant my doppelganger is preparing to use.

He's on a show called *Firing Line* on the Superhero News Network. I rewind to the beginning of the segment and prepare myself for what is coming next.

The female moderator, Kristi Haase, does the introduction. "Joining us now is Cal Stringel, bestselling author, former member of the Gulf Coast Guardians, and the self-proclaimed D-List Supervillain. Thank you for joining us today."

"It's good to be here."

Steve Caldwell, the more confrontational of the two, gives the imposter roughly two seconds before he starts in on him. "Let's talk about what happened in Mexico. Heroes, Villains, Manglers, and a good deal of death. Give us your thoughts, Cal."

"The first word I'd use begins with cluster, but I won't finish the rest, Steve. It's obvious that Devious's people had advance warning—corrupt government officials or corrupt heroes. Take your pick."

"Surely, you're not implying that one of the members of the teams . . ."

"I don't know, Steve. Thing is, you don't know either. Nobody knows."

Kristi tries to be the voice of reason. "But it's also possible that the General had the warning of a psychic. She's been known to consult them in the past."

"True," the imposter concedes. "Either way, the results speak for themselves. Hundreds died. Hundreds more were turned into Manglermals, and there's a twenty-mile quarantine zone in the middle of northern Mexico. I don't even want to talk about what happened to José. He was one of the few Guardians I got along with. Now, instead of clones, he makes animal people."

"Have you reached out to him?"

"He took my call and we had a brief conversation. If we can work out our schedules, we hope to meet somewhere and catch up."

That piques my interest. José knows I'm really alive. I'll have to ask Wendy if she's arranging a trap.

The fake continues, "Meanwhile, I sit here and watch Hera and Athena try and tell the world that it was a successful mission. That's the same thinking that I criticized in my book. I'm really starting to wonder what their definition of successful is."

"But Cal," Kristi says. "That's a pretty broad brush you're painting the situation with. Surely you know that out in the field, things don't always go as planned."

"Then they need better plans! Look at their recent track record."

"I think you're skewing things here, Cal. They captured one of General Devious's bases. Aphrodite, by herself, stabilized the situation in the Philippines. I could—wait. Wait! There's something coming in. I'm getting something from my producers."

Steve is holding his hand to his earpiece, looking confused. "What are we seeing?"

The screen shifts to a football field that looks like a fireworks display went off wrong, and there is a cloud covering the area.

A figure, in what looks like a torn marching band uniform, staggers into view, while the audio mikes pick up screams and cries for help. Having seen quite a bit of it recently, I recognize someone in the throes of a Manglermal transformation.

"There was a detonation during the halftime show. We're not sure what's happening?"

I mute the audio feed and run upstairs. Andy is already switching over to the feed from the news channel. "I think Devious just used one of her bombs in Philadelphia! Alert everyone!"

It takes a few minutes for everyone to assemble. Wendy has to settle Gabby down. Larry and Stacy have to come down from the house. Bobby emerges from the bathroom and I'm not sure I want to know what just went on in there. I can only hope that the air filters in there are up to the task.

By then, the channel that previously broadcast the Army-Navy game is now broadcasting from their central news desk with a news anchor hurriedly rushed into the chair. Andy is pulling the prior footage and trying to enhance it.

Andy works the controls with deft movements across the display panels "I will attempt to draw footage from satellites and any other telemetry I can gather."

We're treated to a fast-moving display of social media whirring and combining into a panoramic picture of the stadium. The marching bands move in formation while the scrolling bar recaps the action from the first half. There is a loud noise that causes all the performers to scatter. It shifts to someone's cellphone capturing a detonation releasing a cloud. All hell breaks loose as the scenes shift from phones to the stadium cameras to the blimp floating above.

"Where's Mega?" Wendy demands.

Andy replies, "At top speed and with assistance from the Jetstream, ETA is five hours to Philadelphia."

Stacy moves close and grabs my hand. "I have to go," she says quietly.

It's the part of the deal she signed up for. I get it. She's out in the limelight and that's exactly where I don't want to be. "I'll ride up with you."

"Wait," Andy interrupts. "This video first appeared on social media web sites seventeen minutes ago. It appears that these accounts are either hacked or they were created and then left dormant until they were needed. It is a broadcast message from General Devious."

The how doesn't matter so much at this point.

There on the computer screen, grinning at the world, is Elaine Davros. Aside from her usual hovering chair, she's wearing an Air Force baseball cap. Using her telekinesis, she waves a series of small pennants in the air around her.

"As a former Air Force Academy graduate, I've always loathed the Army-Navy football game. So, go Falcons! Too bad the president missed the game today. It makes me wonder if he had a tip from those psychics our tax dollars pay for. Too bad he didn't extend that warning to all the others attending that game. Looks like the Secretary of Defense was there. Who knows what that sniveling worm turned into? With the mascots being goats and mules, I wonder how many of those we will get."

She gives a throaty laugh and floats a glass of champagne to her lips. "So that was an amazing halftime show, wasn't it? All those screams. Even thinking about it sends chills up my spine. How about those transformations? It is a pity that Doctor Mangler isn't here to witness his weapon of mass evolution unleashed. Tens of thousands of Manglermals created in one fell swoop, and most of them created from the best and the brightest young officers of two military branches. Now what will our president do? He promises that he will take care of our military, but what about those treaties we've signed with all those other countries banning Manglermals in the armed forces? Quite the dilemma, wouldn't you say?

"Allow me to offer a solution: Bow down to me. It's really that simple. I have a significant inventory of these bombs and the capacity to make more. Maybe I should detonate one in DC? It would show the American people what base animals represent them in Congress. Even more importantly, who would ever vote a person turned into a Mangler back into office? But maybe I should just leave those cowering maggots that we call politicians alone. There are so many ways to take away their precious power and put them on their knees before me. Consider what would happen to the stock markets if New York City were to experience an unprecedented outbreak in animal behavior. Do you really think the Olympians, the Guardians, or even those Renegades can stop me? They must have felt so proud when they captured that one minor base of mine. I salute you for winning the battle while I was winning the war. Well done indeed—very well done."

Devious stops and offers a polite but insincere clap while her eyes practically glow with megalomania. "Victory is so sweet. I would normally demand an immediate surrender, but who doesn't enjoy a good spectacle? My advisors all say that everyone will need an adjustment period to prepare themselves for the new regime. I think a month is appropriate. So, to my future subjects of this and every other country, I hereby give you permission to riot, loot, hoard, burn everything down, head for the hills, flee the cities, settle old grudges, take what is yours, and get whatever you need out of your system. At the end of that month, I will come to claim what is rightfully mine. Do try to spare someone to formally surrender to me. Right now, the world is my oyster, and if you're not careful, you could be one, too."

Her internet transmission ends with a sinister rendition of "Hail to the Chief."

Larry stands up. His jaw is firmly set, and for the first time since he killed Mangler and company, he looks like he's ready to get back out there. "She needs to die. I'll kill that bitch myself, if you need me to."

"I ain't got no problem with offing her. What's got you wound up, big guy?" Bobby asks.

"Stacy said that there's a chance one of my kids was in Philly recently."

"It'll be OK, Larry," Stacy says, trying to reassure him. "I'm sure your child was nowhere near there."

All eyes turn to Wendy. She's the only one other than Stacy who might put a stop to this talk of killing Devious.

"She's gone too far this time. I won't object if it comes to that." Wendy looks to my girlfriend. "Are you going to keep your team out of our way?"

"She's trying to take over countries and destroying lives in the process. Even if that bomb had a ninety percent survival rate, she probably just killed six or seven thousand people. I can't speak for the rest of my team, but I don't object. In fact, the politicians might tie my team's hands and make us sit this one out. You could be our best hope, maybe our only hope. I've seen what you guys are capable of, and I know you'll rise to this challenge as well."

"Damn straight!" Larry says, while Bobby nods in agreement.

In my mind, I take Stacy's words a step further. If the politicians feel truly threatened, they might have the Olympians and the Guardian teams try to stop us.

Wendy catches my eye. She looks far older than a woman in her early twenties has any right to. She's worried, and her fear is obvious. Fear that our fall will rival our sudden rise, fear that things are rapidly approaching the point of no return, and fear that while Devious is playing her hand, the Overlord is still out there waiting for his turn with something just as heinous. The stakes are high, and our margin for error just shrunk to nothing. If we have to pay the piper, the world will suffer alongside us.

• • •

Cal Stringel and the New Renegades will return in *Fall of a D-List Supervillain.*

• • •

About the Author

Jim Bernheimer is the author of several novels and the publisher and editor of three anthologies. He lives in Chesapeake, Virginia with his wife and two daughters while writing whatever four out of the five voices in his head agree on. Visit his website at www.jimbernheimer.com.

Other Books by the Author

Horror, Humor, and Heroes Volume I

Horror, Humor, and Heroes Volume II

Horror, Humor, and Heroes Volume III

Horror, Humor, and Heroes Volume IV

Dead Eye: Pennies for the Ferryman

Dead Eye 2: The Skinwalker Conspiracies

Spirals of Destiny Book One: Rider

Spirals of Destiny Book Two: Sorceress

Prime Suspects: A Clone Detective Mystery

Origins of a D-List Supervillain

Confessions of a D-List Supervillain

Secrets of a D-List Supervillain

The best is yet to come!

Made in the USA
Middletown, DE
19 November 2017